THE WOODS

STEPHEN LEIGH

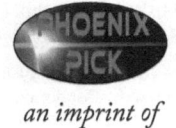

an imprint of

Rockville, Maryland

ISBN: 978-1-61242-096-7

www.PhoenixPick.com
Great Science Fiction & Fantasy
Free Ebook Every Month

Published by Phoenix Pick
an imprint of Arc Manor
P. O. Box 10339
Rockville, MD 20849-0339
www.ArcManor.com

To all those who shared the woods with me, back then…
And, as always, to Denise, with whom I've shared far more.

I need to acknowledge the wonderful critiques and suggestions I received from Jane Lindskold, Maureen McHugh, and P. Andrew Miller—without the three of you, this would be a much lesser book. Thank you!

♈

NOW

The woods were still there, the murky shadows beneath the trees shimmering with their old magic, even now, years and decades later. The trees hold a terrible magic and a beautiful magic, both and together.

I saw the mass of leaf-topped crowns beyond the houses as I parked the car across the street from my old house, on what I still thought of as "Mark's side" of the street and just a few houses down from where he'd lived. Even through the bug-smeared windshield, the vision of the trees beyond the houses frightened me, because I knew what it meant. I could hear the whispers in my head; I could see forms gathering unseen. They'd stayed with me even after I'd fled from them so long ago. The ghosts had haunted me ever since that time, and now I'd come back to confront them again.

Getting out of the car took more effort than I'd expected, but then everything took more effort lately. The bang of the closing car door was an explosion. I half-expected faces to crowd the windows of the houses, peering out to see what this intrusion might be, but I saw no one. I took a breath; I leaned against the car and stared at the woods I could glimpse between the houses.

I knew there was only a meager strip of green-clad hills bristling behind the manicured backyards of Cape Cods and ranches, a wooded buffer between this tract and the next suburb to the north, the remnant of an old forest that was now reduced to a patch maybe two miles wide and perhaps four long. Just down the street from where I'd parked, a small creek emerged timidly from a storm drain that allowed it to pass underneath North Crest Drive, then wandered through an oak-walled valley bordered by the backyards of subdivisions built anywhere from the mid-1950s to the early '70s. The creek emptied finally into the larger Cooper Creek, which in its turn fed the Mill Creek at the long end of the woods. The Mill Creek wandered on through the industrial belt of the valley, walled and swathed and restricted to its concrete flood walls until the stream released its turgid waters into the Ohio River, a dozen miles away...

But that had been an impossible distance back when I'd roamed those woods: Mark and I never went exploring much past the confluence of Cooper Creek with the Mill Creek. Our woods stopped there, and thus so did our interest. Now, Cooper Creek's main tributaries are the waste pipes of local small business and industries, but once upon a time not so long ago...

Then the water thrashing between rocks had been sparkling and alive, its source a deep, cold spring just beyond the subdivisions. Then, Cooper Creek—so named because for the longest part of its winding path it parallels the equally winding Cooper Road— was well populated with red-backed salamanders, crawdads, and tadpoles. Minnows glittered: silver sparks in the shallows of the rocky pools, while water striders skated serenely above, and if you were careful and quiet, you might even come upon a fox lapping at the water from the bank.

Of course, part of that may simply be memory embellished with the artificial glow of time. Truth is as elusive as a minnow darting under a rock. Perhaps, if you'll permit a poor pun, I worship a false idyll.

As I turned away from my old house—a pale yellow now instead of the blue with white trim it had been when we'd sold it—a man came out from the smaller house next door that had once been Mr. Bell's. He noticed me standing next to my car as he raised the lid on the mailbox on his porch. I lifted my hand; he returned the wave hesitantly with a fistful of bills, peering in my direction. I wondered if he would think about this stranger on the street and eventually call the police and mention our little interaction, and how long that response might take.

Long enough, I hoped.

I turned away from him and walked up the street toward Mark's house, but I was looking more at what was behind the houses.

You see, these were *our* woods. Not literally, of course—I don't know who actually owned the land; certainly not my parents, with their well-mowed, 40 x 120 miniature fenced kingdom. It was a rare day back then when I wasn't in those woods: after school, weekends, or all day long during the glorious summer vacations. My sneakered feet and those of my friends, especially Mark, scuffed out persistent dirt paths winding underneath the stands of oaks and maples and through the tangled blackberry brambles, and rarely did we spy other human intruders in our green-roofed world. We ran through the thick underbrush of summer; collected the acorns, buckeyes, and walnuts that fell onto the dry carpeting of dappled autumn leaves; slid through the crisp winter landscape, all black limbs and white snow; rejoiced in the slow rebirth of spring and the slow awakening of frogs, toads, and salamanders from hibernation.

No matter who held legal title to them, those woods were mine—my refuge, my playground, my stage, my school—and they shaped me more than I shaped them. I was fifteen, nearly sixteen, when all that changed, when I found that magic had its other, darker, side as well.

When I found that there were more realities than the one I thought I knew.

It was the day I had to tell Mark that I was moving away. It was the day the world did a lumbering dance and tore itself open around me.

It was 1970.

CHAPTER ONE

Mark Dyson had been my best friend since the third grade, when his family first moved into the house across the street from ours. Mark and I...we were both creatures of the woods: different but complimentary species. He was the stiff oaken branch to my bending willow. In eighth grade art class, Sister Rose Julie had made us draw portraits of our best friends. I'd drawn Mark, of course. His hair had been an easy identifier; all I had to do was mix red and yellow poster paint until it resembled the orange of a pumpkin. But in a painting I couldn't capture his quick speech, or the way his body was always in motion as if some raging fire inside him might reduce him to a cinder if he stood still too long. When we moved on to high school—we both attended Archbishop Mueller High School—Mark moved easily into the role of class clown, a charming troublemaker who made the Marianist Brothers smile even as they gave him demerit slips or sent him to detention in the vice principal's office. He was a teenager whose wilder, manic edges would—now—almost certainly have been ground down by an ADHD diagnosis and a prescription drug supplemented by therapy.

The day things changed, in the summer between our freshman and sophomore years, we met in the woods as always—down in the creek valley where we couldn't hear the constant white noise of cars and lawnmowers. I'd been away with my family for a week. I'd told everyone, including Mark, that the trip was a vacation: wishful thinking on my part, since I knew that wasn't the reason.

My dad had been sent to Pittsburgh for his final promotion interview; after his meeting with a vice president of the company ("Just a formality," Mom had told me. "Your dad has the job if he wants it…") we'd spent the week being shepherded around the city by a realtor, looking for houses. The house to which we'd finally been steered was far larger than the two-bedroom ranch we had on North Crest: a fake Victorian set in an equally artificial new subdivision, the rolling hills bulldozed bare and covered with sod so new you could still see the strips. No trees; at least no old ones. The yard had five or six tiny saplings staked tightly to the lawn as if the landscapers were afraid they might blow away in the next good breeze. The yard was easily three times the size of our current one, unshaded except by the house itself. I could imagine the sweat that would soak my shirt as I mowed it. The house was, the realtor said, in a "truly desirable neighborhood with easy access to the city." When I complained about the lack of any wooded area in the swarm of asphalt streets and newly-seeded lawns, the man rolled his eyes at my parents and favored me with an oily smile. "Well, there's a great park just two streets over. Two ball fields, tennis courts, swimming pool. You can drive to the shopping center or the theater in fifteen minutes flat. And there's tons of restaurants and businesses just looking for kids like you to work in 'em. Just what you're gonna need, eh, buddy?"

My parents nodded in tandem with the realtor, and I knew that no argument I might make would prevail. "When we move here, and when you turn sixteen, we'll get you that car you want," Mom whispered to me. "With the raise your Dad's getting, we can loan you the money until you find a job here." Dad signed the preliminary paperwork and we drove back to Cincinnati.

I'd headed for the woods as soon as the suitcases were unloaded, knowing I'd find Mark there. I was already feeling guilty. Over the years, there had been very little I hadn't told Mark or shared with him, but I'd never mentioned this impending promotion of Dad's even though I'd known about it for two weeks or more. I'd thought that—maybe, somehow—if I never talked about it that it wouldn't happen. I was afraid that actually *saying* the words to Mark would crystallize them and make them real.

Despite the July heat, it was cool under the leaves, an emerald twilight interrupted by brilliant wedges of sunlight that only made the shade darker. He was standing in one of the pollen-dusted sun shafts, and I could see him clearly. "Jeez," I said to him, all the words I'd prepared forgotten as I squinted at him, shading my eyes with one hand. "What happened to your face?"

A mottled bruise purpled Mark's left cheekbone, his skin just turning a sickly yellow-green around the edges, and his eye on that side swollen and dark. Mark scowled and touched the cheek gingerly. "I walked into a fucking wall a couple nights ago. Thought I could get to the john without turning on the damn lights. Guess I was wrong." He tilted his head. "Does it look that bad?"

"It's not too bad," I told Mark, a polite lie. Frankly, his bruise was as obvious as a turd on ice cream. And there was also the lie of omission: I knew immediately that his explanation was an evasion, but I didn't call him on it. Over the years, Mark had "fallen" or "walked into a door" or "slipped" dozens of times. I thought for a long while that he was simply the clumsiest person I knew, a trait made all the more strange considering how easily he moved through the woods. I knew—or suspected—better now. "Hurt much?"

"Shit, yeah." Mark had taken up profanity more and more over the last few years, sprinkling his conversations with vulgarities that sounded a little too forced, though he still judiciously deleted the expletives around adults. When Mark started cursing, I'd started to do the same, but the purple words were still fingernails down the blackboard of my Catholic upbringing, sounding false and uneasy. For a long time, my voice quavered perceptively when I said them, as if I expected our parish priest, Father Brautski, to suddenly appear in front of me, spouting hellfire and damnation for my sins. "It sure hurt like hell when it happened," Mark shrugged. That much I believed. "C'mon, we're wasting the goddamn day talking."

With that, he headed off down the trail, leaving me no chance to broach my news. We had no plans—but then we rarely had plans anymore. In years past, we'd often entered the woods prepared and provisioned like an expedition, with buckets for tadpoles and jars for salamanders, bearing air rifles for playing army or kite-string-laced bows, or sticks thrust through belts for mock sword fights. To enter the shadows under the leaves of oak, sycamore, maple, and buckeyes was to pass through a portal into another world. Once there, we were no longer children: we metamorphosed into characters snared in a web of tales cobbled together from the musty pages of books and the brightly colored lines of comics, from the dark and mysterious caverns of movie houses and the black-and-white landscape of old television shows. We could be treading the hillsides of an alien world under trees with silver trunks and orange leaves, or the unsettled wilderness of Daniel Boone's time. We'd lived in our imaginations for years, Mark and I; we were heroes and villains and lost princes destined to regain their thrones. But...

In the last year or so, reality had begun to intrude. I spent less time in the woods and more at home. I was learning to play guitar and I was listening to new music. I was dreaming of playing rock and roll, of being one of those singers on the posters I'd taped to the walls of my room. I was also starting to write down some of the stories that prowled in my head rather than just playing at them. I'd even looked for a job after school let out, though no one wanted to hire me.

Snared in the acne-riddled landscape of pubescence, I was beginning to feel self-conscious abandoning myself to fantasy; but not Mark.

Not Mark.

Once in the woods, Mark—still...always...—became someone else.

We could both manage the play-acting transformation, where in our mind's eye we became Robin Hood or Geronimo as soon as we stepped through the brush at the edge of the woods. But this...this new person who entered Mark's body was someone else, someone more feral and dark and—contradictorily—adult. I saw the metamorphosis happen now as we moved down the steep hill toward the creek. The slow mutation was all in small things, in the way he held himself. His usual manic gaiety dissolved in the cool, green air. The lines of his mouth turned down and his eyes narrowed. He appeared darker and heavier, wrapped in a mood that cloaked him like a drifting fog. I didn't quite know who Mark was, then; didn't know who he was becoming, or why.

I wasn't quite sure I liked this Mark. I know I didn't like the way this new personality made me feel awkward and adolescent, prone to saying something I knew Mark would consider stupid.

Mark stopped suddenly, listening carefully as he peered into a hollow bearded with ferns. "There," he said. "Did you hear that?"

"What? I don't hear anything."

"*Listen*, then…" Then, he shook his head. "No, they're gone now. Damn…"

"Who's gone?" I asked. "A deer?" I laughed. "Wolves?" Sometimes we pretended that we'd glimpsed wolves or bears in the shadows of the trees—creatures that might have walked here a century or more ago but hadn't been seen in decades. Once or twice, I would have sworn that I'd truly seen them. Now, I knew we'd only been fooling ourselves.

Mark glanced at me, and I wasn't sure what I saw in those eyes, the same color as the leaves around us. "You're fucking deaf, Rob, you know that? Sometimes you're just like the rest of them—they come through here and they don't even *see*."

"I can see, Mark," I told him. "I can see just fine. What's eating you, asshole?" (Yes, my voice quavered. No, Father Brautski did not appear.)

Mark grimaced. I thought for a moment that his anger, as combustible as his moods, was going to flare. His hands fluttered at his hips, then dropped. "Nothing," he said finally. "Fucking nothing. Look, why don't we head up towards Seven Caves? We haven't been there at all this summer."

It sounded fine to me. The Seven Caves weren't caves at all, but a grove of young soft maples we'd discovered, roofed over with a tangled web of vines that were slowly strangling the trees. The vines created a maze of several low "rooms" as they wove in and out through the branches of the trees—rooms that would change from season to season and year to year as the vines grew and died. We'd found the grove four years before, and it had become a pirate lair, a Nazi-held Rhine castle, a hidden dungeon, a set of underground caverns toothed with stalactites, all in turn. Autumn always eventually eroded the leafy roofs and walls, and we'd abandon it until the next spring. Most of the other kids in the neighborhood were a year or two older than us; one by one they'd given up the woods for more adult mysteries. When the caves had bloomed the last two years, they'd done so alone.

Except for Mark. Except for me. We both still could find fantasy in the woods, even if those fantasies were fast becoming more adult in tone.

I followed Mark as he moved easily along the trail. I envied his long stride, the nonchalant way he slid around branches or found the least difficult path through the brambles. He was fluid and graceful here, at home in the mock wilderness. I could always imagine Mark as an Indian scout—in fact, it was a role he'd often played in younger days—a quiet whisper moving through the forest, seeing everything but rarely being seen himself. I was, in contrast, more the lumbering bear, bulling my way through tangles and being tripped by mischievous tree roots. In a few minutes, I was sweating and breathing heavily trying to keep up with Mark, who had already vanished somewhere in the half-gloom ahead. The Seven Caves were over the creek, across a small ridge and on the other side of a small field created by a lightning-strike fire several years before. Mark was there a good minute before I arrived, leaning against a sycamore with his head tilted appraisingly. He watched as I thrashed my way through the high grass and thorns, blinking at the sudden sunlight.

The bruise was a dark blotch on his face. "You're slow," he said.

"I'm deliberate," I answered, wiping sweat away with the sleeves of my tee. Mark's grin flashed over his face and vanished again. "Hey Mark, listen," I began. "I've got something I have to…" but he was gone again, ducking under a low portal of leaves and into the labyrinth. I grimaced and shook my head, and—again—followed.

Mark was waiting for me in the first room. Here, the vines snared a ring of saplings and wound around one of the parent trees of the grove, lacing overhead so low that we could barely stand upright. He was staring up to where the sunlight broke on the foliage, and as soon as I entered the room, he was moving again, stooping over and waving me further into the vine-cloaked labyrinth. "It's changed since last year," he said. "Remember how this room was larger last time we were here, and there was a passage over there that's gone now. Nothing ever stays the same." His head came down. He was staring at me, his eyebrows wedged over narrowed eyes. "Except us," he continued. It was more a command than a statement. "You and me."

Those words caught my stomach and twisted. I wiped at my forehead again, wishing he'd look away from me. I wished I'd made myself tell him before, the moment I'd seen him. I wish I'd told him before we left last week, or a month ago when my Dad first broached the subject of a possible move. It had colored all our interactions since the end of school. In the last week of school, Mark had found a summer job bussing tables at Maury's Diner, down the hill from our subdivision, but I never told him why Maury turned me down, as did all the rest of the places to which I applied. *"Sorry, but if you're going to be moving soon, I can't use you..."* If Mark suspected something, he'd never mentioned it, either.

"Mark—" I began, but then he turned and slid through an opening I didn't remember.

"Come on," his voice tugged at me. "You fucking gotta see this. I found it while you were away..."

I followed, through another smaller room, then squeezing through a tiny gap in the vines. Suddenly I was outside the "caves," in a mature stand of oaks and buckeyes. Mark was a few yards away, posing in front of two piles of stones about six feet apart. "Take a look," he said.

I glanced at Mark, then at the stones. Someone—I assume it had been Mark—had cleared away the brush from them. I stooped down in front of the nearest pile, suddenly intrigued. I swept a hand across the stones: they were smooth, polished granite, a variety I'd never seen around here, and they'd been roughly cut into six-inch high slabs and fitted together without mortar. The twin piles, about hip-high to the two of us, were the only remnants of whatever had once been here. I glanced around to see if there were other blocks laying around, but didn't see any.

"Can't you *feel* it, man?" Mark was asking me. "I mean, can't you just feel how old these are?"

I shrugged. "Yeah, I guess. Miss Flynn told us last year that there were settlers here in the late 1700s, so I guess…"

"Shit, Rob," Mark spat. "You don't feel *nothing*. How can you think it was goddamn 'settlers'…" He was pacing now, back and forth between the two piles. "This is fucking *old*, Rob. Ancient."

"What, like the Indian mounds up in Lebanon? Maybe, but I don't think—"

"*No!*" Exasperated, Mark shouted the word. I heard the denial echo faintly from the hills. He held his hands out, as if warming them over an invisible fire. "Something else. Something…I don't know what. But I can *feel* it. There was power here in the ruins, Rob. This is—was—a gateway. Look at it; can't you imagine how it must have looked, centuries ago? Hell, a thousand years ago."

"A gateway…" I suddenly knew what this was—another game for us to play, a wonderful imaginary adventure like the thousand others we'd had before over the years. In the right mood, I'd have gone right along with him, and we'd have entered a fantasy where stepping between the two rock piles would transport us to a medieval world where we battle imaginary dragons and search for the White Wizard of the Endless Forest, at least until it was time to go home for supper. It wasn't a game I wanted to play right now. I felt far too old for it and the confession I needed to make was pressing too hard against my chest. I took a long breath. "Mark, man, I gotta—"

"We can open it again," he interrupted. "I know we can. We'll go through, and—" He slapped his hand down on one of the piles of stone and at the same time clutched at my shoulder. He must have hit the nerve, because I felt a shock run through my arm like I'd touched a live electrical circuit. I grunted in pain and stepped back, shrugging his hand away from me and trying to shake out the tingling in my fingers. The pain made me angry.

"Mark, listen to me, would you, damn it!" I shouted, and he stopped in mid-phrase, swinging around. The explanation started to tumble out in fitful, erratic spurts while all the time he watched me, his mouth tightening. "While you were gone…There isn't anything I can do about it…My dad, his company made him this offer…" I staggered to a shrugging halt. "Man, I don't know how else to say it. I'm *moving*, Mark. To Pittsburgh. The sign'll be in our yard in a few days."

Mark didn't say anything, but the bruise on his face went darker and a flush slid up his neck and onto his cheeks. He just watched me, and I had to look away, my hands waving helplessly. My fingers still had prickles. "I tried to tell you before, Mark. But you didn't give me a chance. I'm sorry. I really am."

He nodded once, silent. He was looking somewhere past me.

"What do you want me to say, Mark? I don't like this, either. Hell, I kept hoping it'd change, that Dad's promotion would fall through, but it didn't. We're...*leaving*. I don't have a choice."

"I thought you were my friend," he said. Tendons drew ridges in his neck and bunched at his jaw line. I'd never seen his face look like that; his eyes were pouched and dark, and I could see the high ridge of his cheekbones. His skin looked as if it had been pasted over his skull, drawn and tight. "I guess I was wrong, huh?"

"This doesn't have anything to do with our being friends," I said desperately, hating the open hurt I could hear in his voice, and at the same time feeling the defensive anger rise inside me, feeding on my guilt. After all, I really *didn't* have a choice; if it were Mark's parents moving away, it would be the same for him. But it wasn't Mark who was leaving; it was *me* and he stared as if I'd deliberately chosen to go. "C'mon, Mark, that's not fair. There's nothing I can do. You understand that, don't you? I can't do anything to change this, as much as I want to. Dad's got this better job..." I shrugged. "We're moving as soon as Mom can sell the house. Definitely by the end of the summer."

He sniffed. His hands fisted at his side. "I don't need you, Rob. I don't fucking need you at all. I can do this on my own."

"Do *what*? Haven't you been listening to me?"

He started to turn away from me, and I reached out to stop him. I don't know what I thought I could do—I wanted to appease his anger; I wanted to let him know that I understood what he was feeling, but I knew immediately that I'd made the wrong choice. "Get the hell away from me!" Mark shouted. "What the fuck are you, some goddamn queer?" He plucked my hand from his shoulder, and then took a roundhouse cut at my face that missed by a scant inch as I ducked my head back. I realized that if I hadn't moved, he *would* have hit me, hit me with his full strength. The realization stunned me. Sure, Mark and I had squabbled over the years. We'd tussled with each other a few times, but even at our most angry we'd always seemed to realize that there was an unspoken limit.

Not now. Mark had lashed out with the intent to hurt me as much as he could. He'd struck at me like an enemy. I stared at him, mesmerized by the realization. "Mark—"

"*Fuck* you, Rob!" he shouted at me with his mouth wide, leaning forward. "Just…fuck you." He was trembling, his whole body shaking. Mine was too; I could feel my own muscles shivering and I realized that I was scared. I didn't know what would happen if Mark came at me now. His eruption of unexpected fury was frightening. He was a mad beast hovering on the edge of an attack, and I braced myself, involuntarily backing away from him with my hands up. I was aware of how much bigger than me Mark was, of the corded muscles in his arms.

And just as suddenly, with a wordless, guttural shout, he turned and ran back the way we'd come, ducking under the screening vines and disappearing. I could hear him thrashing through the leaves. I just stood there, listening to the residual adrenaline buzzing in my ears and shaking my head.

After a few minutes, when I couldn't hear Mark any more, I headed home myself, wondering what had happened and blaming myself.

CHAPTER TWO

"…know he always drinks more than's good for him."

"But that doesn't excuse…Rob, that you?"

I came in the back door, as usual, and heard my parents speaking together in the front room, a conversation that cut off abruptly when I let the screen door slam.

Still angry and confused by Mark's attack in the woods, I wasn't much in the mood to talk. "Yeah. What's up?"

Dad came in with Mom trailing slightly behind. I remember thinking that Dad was starting to look old to me—not just the generic "old" label that every kid puts on his parents, but tired and worn down and graying. I thought at the time that it was just a result of the trip, residual exhaustion from his interviews and finding houses. I'd realize later just how worried my Dad was about this move, about what awaited him in his new position, about having the bottom-line responsibility for a new division. He might have discussed his concerns with Mom (or maybe not), but never with me. I knew Mom sold houses—"And I can do that anywhere," I remember her saying to Dad once—but I wasn't entirely sure exactly what my father did. He worked for Procter & Gamble, which he sometimes referred to jokingly as "Procter & God." That was all I knew, which was my fault. It was all I'd ever really wanted to know.

Whatever my folks had just been talking about, the subject had bothered them. Mom slid into one of the kitchen chairs; Dad leaned against the buffet. The good china—used twice a year,

Thanksgiving and Christmas—rattled behind him. "You been with Mark?" he asked, in a far too casual voice.

"Yeah." I'd long ago perfected the monosyllabic conversation, the eternal standard for teenagers when talking to their parents. I gave them unadorned, solitary droppings for replies, never answering more than I had to. In their turn, they rarely shared with me their reasons for asking endless questions.

Dad nodded, as if pondering layers of meaning in my single word answer; Mom inspected her fingernails as if she could see the reflection of her Jackie Kennedy bob, now more than half a decade out of fashion, in the glossy red surfaces. "How was Mark?"

"Fine." I added a careful shrug and went to the refrigerator. I let the cool air slide over me, feeling their gazes on my back. Dad's voice came to me over the hum of the fan motor.

"Joe Bell tells us that Mark got…hurt while we were away."

"Yeah?" Joe Bell was our next-door neighbor: an ancient widower, retiree, and WWI veteran who had nothing better to do than sit on his porch all day and watch the neighborhood, and who told everyone what he'd seen at great length. He had an elderly dachshund bitch that was named, for some reason I could never fathom, "Kitty-Kitty." From my interactions with the man, his sense of humor might have been surgically removed. His dachshund had a mean temperament; she snapped and barked at anyone who passed. I think all the kids on the street had been nipped by the dog at one point or another. Joe Bell snapped at us kids as often as his dog, growling and grumbling whenever a ball rolled into his yard. I didn't like the man. I didn't like the way he nosed into everyone else's business. I especially didn't like him nosing about in mine.

I snagged a Coke from the shelf and let the door close. I popped the lid and took a sip, underhanding the tab in the general direction of the garbage can. It hit the edge and dropped to the linoleum. Neither of my parents seemed to notice, so I didn't bother to pick it up. I wiped my mouth and rolled the cold aluminum across my forehead. I looked back at my parents. I waited; they waited. "So how's Mark?" Dad asked.

I took a sip of the Coke and lifted a shoulder. "Mark's got a bruise, that's all. He's OK, though," I added. "No big deal." I could have given them the rest of the explanation. I didn't.

Some silent communication passed between my parents, and they both nodded. "What's up?" I asked again.

Dad sighed, Mom watched Dad. "Nothing," he said. "It's just…" I waited, taking another sip. "Mr. Bell was saying there was a lot of shouting over at the Dyson house yesterday."

I'd also perfected my shrugs. I gave them the one that meant "and your point?" Loud arguments, sometimes punctuated with crashes and thuds, were nothing new at Mark's house. Everyone in the neighborhood heard Jason Dyson—"JD" to his few friends— when he yelled at Mark or his sisters or his mom. I always thought Mark's mom looked like a brown-haired mouse, always peering around as if she were afraid that a cat was about to leap on her from some hidden corner. Jason Dyson's volume was usually directly related to the number of beers he'd consumed—which told me who my parents had been talking about when I'd come in. I took another sip of the Coke.

"Rob…" Mom began, then stopped. She glanced at my Dad once more.

"What?"

"Just…umm….if Mark told you anything important, something that we needed to know, you'd tell us, wouldn't you?"

"Sure." The agreement came easily, because I knew they expected it. I wondered if they actually believed me.

"I mean, you're his best friend, and he needs you, at least while you're still here. He didn't tell you anything today, did he? About how he…hurt himself?"

"Said he walked into a door. In the night. Just a stupid thing."

My parents consulted silently once more, then they both nodded. "OK, Rob," Dad said. "Thanks."

Oh sure, I knew perfectly well what they were implying; I just wasn't going to admit it. I gave them another shrug (the one meaning "I guess we're done now?") and went on up to my room. I lay down across my bed and stared up at the ceiling, dotted with luminescent, stick-on stars in the patterns of the constellations—

a legacy from my interest in astronomy three years before. Jimi Hendrix and Jim Morrison stared at me from the walls.

I could easily imagine Jason Dyson hitting Mark hard enough to give him a shiner—I know he'd never been reluctant to swat his children hard on the backside when they'd done something he didn't like. It wasn't much of a leap to see him getting angry and out of control enough to hit Mark with his fist.

I could also imagine that if our positions were reversed, if it had been me with the bruised face, I might have lied about it, too. Maybe. Probably, even.

I remembered a backyard barbecue at the Dysons', back when I was seven or eight. We'd finished eating; our mothers were at the picnic table in the backyard, putting things away. Mark and I went to toss a baseball in the driveway. "See if you can catch *this*," Mark said to me, and uncorked a fast and wild pitch that sailed well over my head. We all heard the tinkling of glass as the garage window shattered. JD had come storming over and walloped Mark on the backside as I winced with each open-handed strike: once, twice, three times. "Now, you get the broom and clean up that mess, you hear me, boy? And this comes out of your allowance. You got that?" Mark, sniffing but refusing to cry in front of me, stalked off into the house while JD went back to the deck as I stared after him, my mouth open in surprise and shock. My dad set his beer on the railing; I could see him frowning.

"Kids break things, JD," Dad said, his voice ominously quiet, the way it got when he was really angry. "It was just an accident. Hitting him doesn't accomplish anything."

JD glared at my dad. His face was blotched with red, his thinning hair disheveled. I saw the fists his hands made at his side, and wondered whether he and my dad were going to fight. Mark's Mom was watching with her hand at her mouth, shaking her head a little but not moving; my Mom got up from the picnic table and put her hand on my Dad's arm.

"He's my kid," JD retorted. " I don't tell you how to raise yours."

"I don't care. Hitting your kid like that—" Dad noticed me watching, swallowed whatever he was going to say, and grimaced.

"Rob," he called. "Why don't you go help Mark find a broom and clean up the mess."

"OK," I told him, glad for the excuse to leave. I don't know what happened after that, though I recall that we went back to our house not much later. For a few weeks, I noticed that Mark's dad was quieter around us when I came over to play with Mark.

For a few weeks.

In the last year or so, Mark had started saying things about his parents that made me uncomfortable. He claimed that he hated them, using words that made me shudder because I had a hard time even thinking them myself, saying that his dad was a "fucking asshole" and his mother a "stupid cunt"; that as soon as he was eighteen he was going to leave if he didn't leave sooner; that if his dad so much as touched him again, he'd goddamn kill him. Everything was hyperbole with Mark lately; his world had gone to stark black and white, all the shades of life shifting all the way to one side or the other: right or wrong. I'd figured it was just Mark, that like me he was awash in the adolescent hormonal tides that made *everything* seem a little crazy at times. After all, I swore—under my breath, at least—that I hated my parents at least once a day.

Now I wondered if there wasn't more for Mark.

My mom's words kept coming back to me: ...*he needs you...* Somehow I knew she was right. I figured I'd give Mark the rest of the day to cool off, then talk to him tomorrow. Maybe by then he'd be ready to tell me the truth. Maybe by then we could talk about what was going to happen when I left.

Mark wasn't at his house the next morning. I was relieved when Mark's sister Jackie answered my knock instead of Mrs. Dyson. Jackie was eight; she told me she didn't know where Mark had gone, only that he'd left the house before she got up.

"Where'd he go?"

She shook her head. "Don't know."

"Who is it, damn it?" I heard Jason Dyson bellow from the kitchen as Jackie started to close the door—I wondered what he was doing home in the daytime when every other father in the neighborhood was at work, but I also wasn't going to stick around to find out. I thanked Jackie and left before JD decided to come and see who it was for himself. I bolted down the concrete steps at a leap and across the lawn.

Next door to the Dyson house was the Schmidts'. Pete Schmidt, seventeen and the envy of the teenagers in the neighborhood because he actually owned his own car, an old and rusty VW Beetle, was in the driveway changing the spark plugs. He told me that a bunch of the guys were going to have a pick-up baseball game at Hilltop Park this afternoon and to tell Mark if I saw him, but no, he didn't know where Mark was. He'd been out there all morning—if Mark had come out the front door, Pete insisted, he would have noticed him.

I knew then where Mark had gone—if not specifically, at least in general—because it was where I would have gone myself. I cut through the vacant lot next to the Schmidt house and slipped under the trees waiting there. Once in the woods, I splashed down the creek to the pocked, glacial-deposited boulder Mark and I had dubbed Salamander Hill. I checked the muddy ground there: yes, the print of a sneaker tread pressed ridges in the mud, heading away from the creek. Several minutes later, I thought I could hear Mark's voice as I maneuvered through the passageways of the Seven Caves. Even though I couldn't make out the words, his voice had an odd, rhythmic pattern to it. I didn't call to him, just pushed through the caves until I reached the other side. In my head, I rehearsed what I'd say to him: *Mark, listen, I know your Dad hits you. If you ever want to talk about it...*

Mark was standing between the two piles of stone—his "gateway"—illuminated in a slanting ray of morning sun. He was facing away from me, out toward the deepest part of the woods. I could hear the words now, clichéd and predictable, considering the fantasies in which we'd indulged over the years: "...open the path, I command you..." His voice was half-shout, half-drone.

In that second, everything shifted for me. Mark's upraised hands were streaked with dark rivulets, his left hand held something I couldn't identify, and there were splashes of bright red on the stones to either side of him. A hand axe glittered on the ground at his feet, the steel edge stained with the same color.

I realized belatedly that the red stain was blood, and that there was a frightening amount of it. Sudden fear hammered at my temples and hissed in my ears, and I wanted to run back the way I'd come. If this was a game, Mark had taken it beyond anything we'd played before.

"Shit!" I yelled involuntarily.

Mark whirled around, mouth open in a shout, and more droplets spattered with the movement, a bloody stream arcing toward me. I ducked, my hands covering my head. I felt hot liquid strike my forearms. "Jesus!" I screamed at Mark. "What the hell *is* this?"

"You didn't want to be part of it," Mark spat back at me. "You're leaving, remember." I could see now that he was holding the limp, decapitated body of a dog: Joe Bell's dog Kitty-Kitty, I realized with another start. The dachshund's open eyes stared up at me accusingly from the ground not two feet away from my feet, half-buried in dead leaves.

"Mark, this is totally crazy." I brushed at my arms, and Kitty-Kitty's blood smeared. I stared at the stains, aghast.

"What the hell do you care, Rob? It's not *about* you, not anymore. Get the fuck out of here. This is *mine!*"

I didn't know what to say. I could feel my pulse pounding, could hear the quick thumping of my heart. We'd played at magic, a thousand times before, but the feeling had never been so dark, so visceral as that moment. Mark shook his fist, and the body of Kitty-Kitty wriggled in a mockery of life, the fur damp with her blood, an accusation. My stomach roiled, and I almost gagged. "What are you talking about? *What's* yours, Mark?" I managed to gasp out.

"The gateway. Whatever's beyond it and whatever I can bring here through it. It's mine. It could have been *ours*, Rob, ours, but you..." Mark was almost sobbing, his face contorted, the bruise on his face mottled against his light skin. "*Damn* it, don't you understand, Rob? You're leaving, and I...I need..." He stopped, and with an animal howl flung Kitty-Kitty's body away, the limp brown corpse passing within a few feet of my head. We heard it crash into the underbrush.

"Stop it! Both of you! Just stop it now!"

I will always remember the shock of her first appearance, the utter surreality of her entrance into our lives. She stood maybe ten feet away, deeper in the woods just past Mark's "gateway" of stones. Neither of us had heard her approach; we didn't know how long she'd been there watching. Her imperious command, so totally unexpected, shocked and silenced us both. We turned, and I can still feel the shimmer of disbelief that went through me as I saw her, the second time in the last few minutes that the world utterly changed around me.

She was about our age, fifteen or sixteen, just past the awkward boundary of childhood. Her hair was raven-dark, long, and tangled as if she hadn't brushed it in days. Sweat plastered a few strands to her forehead. She had on a loose blouse that had slipped slightly down one shoulder and betrayed the strap of a bra, and her patched jeans fit snugly over hips widening with dawning womanhood. And her face…She wasn't pretty, not in the cosmetically-enhanced way that many of the girls at school were. Her nose was too wide and so was her mouth, devoid of any lipstick. No nail polish on her fingernails, either, and her hands were as dirt-stained as either of ours. Her eyes were her best feature: ice-pale blue eyes, startling under the unraveling night of her hair—they danced as if the sunlight was striking bright crystal. Not pretty, no…but there was something commanding about her that made her attractive, all the stronger for the inexplicable abruptness of her arrival. She was…different. If we'd been confronted by wolf or bear, dragon or griffin, I could not have been more surprised.

"Who," Mark was already saying, "the fuck are you?"

"Sheila," she answered. "And nice goddamn language. I know *you*," she said as Mark guffawed at her comment. "You're Mark." Her gaze went to me, and I was lost. "And you're Rob," she said.

We were both gaping now. She stepped toward us, moving between the two piles of stones and glancing at the blood-spattered granite as she passed. I watched her face as she noticed the remnants of Mark's blood magic—hell, I was helpless to do anything other than watch, snared by her already—and there was no horror in her eyes, no distaste in the set of her mouth. If she was disturbed by what she saw, she betrayed nothing. If anything, she seemed to smile faintly, and the too-large nostrils of her nose flared. The sharp tang of blood hung in the air.

"You're an awful mess," she told Mark. His hands were covered with red-brown, sticky stains. A spray had splashed across the front of his T-shirt and droplets dappled the front of his jeans. "You need to go clean your hands in the creek, and that shirt too. It won't get all of it out, but you can tell your mother that you had a bloody nose. She'll believe you, because that's what she'll want to believe." The speech came out calmly, easily, as if it were the simplest thing in the world. "Rob will bury Kitty-Kitty while you're cleaning up, then he can clean up a little himself," she continued, and I found myself nodding, agreeing to all this. "No sense in having the body stink up the whole area or having someone find it. Then we'll go back."

She smiled, then, and we both grinned back at her. "It's going to be OK," she told us. "Really it is. I can tell already. Everything's fine now."

CHAPTER THREE

Her name was Sheila Niemann. She, her mother, and two cats had moved into a house on South Crest, the next street over, two days ago. She would be sixteen in less than a month, and would be going to Reading (pronounced "Redding," not "Reeding") High School rather than the local parochial high school for girls. Her mother not only wasn't Catholic, she (and Sheila) didn't believe in any organized religion at all, at least none that Mark or I guessed at, although Sheila claimed that they weren't atheists.

We learned all this walking out of the woods that afternoon. We also learned that her knowledge of adult behavior was keen: as she said they would, both of our mothers accepted the nosebleed story without even flinching. "Look, your parents are going to accept any reasonable explanation for something as long as it allows them to think that nothing out of the ordinary is happening to their kids." She proclaimed that with grim certainty, as if it were a granite-slab truth with which she was intimately familiar.

Neither Mark nor I was quite so certain. "Oh, sure," we replied. "Like that's going to happen." But it did. We went to my house first to clean up the blood, though my Mom's first reaction was a grimace and a suspicious question. "What happened to *you?*" Mark's damp tee and jeans were still liberally dappled with pale bloodstains.

"Rob hit me in the face," Mark said, then grinned at my Mom, who looked at me sternly.

"Robert Paul Mullins, how could you…" she began until Mark started laughing.

"We were going through the woods and a branch I was holding snapped back and got him right in the nose," I told her. "Man, you should have seen it bleed. It even got on me. I thought for sure I'd broken it, but Mark's all right now. See, it's not even swollen." That was the story we'd agreed upon. Actually, it was the story Sheila had suggested we tell. Mom didn't even seem to notice the fact that I was babbling like a kid, instead of giving her my usual terse teenage grunts.

Mark was still grinning, and Mom seemed to realize that Sheila was there for the first time.

"Well, who's this now?" she said. Now she was looking at Sheila, not us, and I couldn't quite decipher the look on her face. Then Sheila smiled at her, and the corners of Mom's mouth lifted in response.

"I'm Sheila Niemann, Mrs. Mullins. My Mom and I just moved in over on South Crest. I love your house, by the way. Just walking into it, I can tell it feels so much more like a home than ours does yet."

I saw the deliberate flattery hit Mom like a velvet fist, following up the initial impact of Sheila's smile. The one-two punch shattered the barrier of suspicion that had somehow flashed into being when Mom had first seen her. "Well, just give it time, Sheila. New homes always take time," she said, and flicked a quick, deliberate glance in my direction. In the presence of her son and a young woman, she seemed to have entirely forgotten the bloodstains on our clothes. "I've sold lots of houses to people just moving into a new city, and I know how tough moving to a new neighborhood is on kids your age," she said, and now she was talking to me more than Sheila. "But after a few months, you'll settle in, I'm sure."

I ignored that. "We're going to the family room, OK?"

Mom hesitated. I saw it. Before this it had always been just Mark and me, but now Sheila had changed the equation. But Sheila was still smiling at her, and finally Mom shrugged. "Fine. Your father went out to the store to pick up groceries for supper. We'll eat around six. Roast chicken sound good?"

"Whatever," I told her. We left her, walking down the hallway and into the back addition to the house, added on just last year, when there was no sign of a promotion and no move in sight.

"Nice room," Sheila said. She ran a hand over the huge bulk of the Zenith console TV—a color set my parents had bought last year. "Your parents must be doing all right."

I shrugged. "Dad's a manager at P&G. Mom's a realtor."

Sheila nodded, looking at the bookcase, her head tilted as she glanced at the titles. "You the science fiction reader, Rob?" she asked, glancing back at me. I nodded, and she turned back to perusing the books, occasionally running her finger down the leather spine of one of the hardbacks.

"Yeah," I told her. "My family likes to read. We used to have a big bookcase in the front room, but Mom had me and Dad take it down a few weeks ago and pack up the books…" I stopped…. *when they decided to move*, was the rest of the sentence, but it wouldn't come out.

"Yeah," Mark said. "Their front room was like a damn library." I shot a warning glance at him for the profanity. "Now I know why the bookcase is gone, huh?"

"Interesting," she said, ignoring Mark's last comment. "Everything from classics to modern. I like that." Mark and I watched her, watched the way she moved, the way she occasionally flicked her unruly hair back. The way her jeans looked on her body. I was beginning to think it wasn't a bad body at all. Most of the girls I knew tried to look like the emaciated models in the magazines. They would have called Sheila—in their generous moments—"a little heavy."

She turned back to us. Frowned. "Mark, you need to wash more of that blood out of your shirt before you get back to your house. I'll bet Rob'll let you borrow a T-shirt."

There was a moment of awkward silence, and I realized that Sheila was looking at me. I lurched back into awareness. "Yeah, no problem," I said to Mark. "You know where they are in my room. Top left drawer of the dresser. Just go ahead and grab one when you're done."

Mark stared, fingering the red-brown dappled cotton of his shirt. I knew he didn't want to leave the room, didn't want me to be alone with her. I could feel the jealousy already, could sense the mental strings he'd already wrapped around Sheila. He looked at her, then at me. "I'll be back in minute," he said. "Less."

"You know he's really upset that you're leaving him," Sheila said after Mark left the room. She moved away from the bookcase and stood close to me. Her breath smelled of cinnamon, and there were flecks of pale gold in the forget-me-not irises of her eyes. "He can't tell you how frightened that makes him, so he's turned it all into anger. You've been his crutch and his support, all along, and now that's being taken away when it feels to him that he needs it more than ever."

I blinked into the torrent of quiet words. "That's a pretty deep psychoanalysis. How long have you known Mark, Dr. Freud?" I said, trying for "scornful" and only managing "perplexed." "An hour now?"

"So am I wrong?" One side of her mouth lifted as if she might smile. "Or am I right?"

She was right. At least I thought she was, but I wasn't going to admit it. "I can't do anything about us leaving," I said. "Dad's going to be staying in Pittsburgh most of the time from now on. Mom and I will follow when the house sells. I don't how long I'll be here. Maybe only a month, but absolutely only for the summer—whether the house sells or not, I'm supposed to start school in Pittsburgh in the fall." I was gesturing and my fingertips brushed the top of her nearly bare shoulder. I must have picked up some static electricity from the carpet in the TV room, because the touch sent a pinprick of electricity through me, and Sheila gave a soft gasp of surprise. We both looked at the tanned skin there, and I put my hands in the pockets of my jeans.

"A month can be a long time." She watched my face. "Long enough for some things." In that moment, I realized that, all along, she had seemed, well, *older*, and I took a step back, disguising my discomfiture with a laugh.

"You know that Mark thinks you're his."

She hadn't moved with me, but she was still watching me. Her eyes narrowed, and her full lips pressed together for a moment. "Really? And why's that?"

"He probably half-believes he brought you here with that crazy sh— …that crazy stuff he was doing out there. So in his mind you sorta belong to him."

"What do you think, Rob?"

I lifted my shoulders and let them fall without taking my hands out of my pockets. "You startled me too, just showing up like that in the middle of things. But you're real enough. I don't think there are any magicians or wizards living over on South Crest. And I figure that you belong to yourself."

She smiled and laughed, a laugh that held summer and sunshine and the smell that comes just after a soft rain.

"I like that," she said. "I like that a lot. You'd better be careful, Rob."

"He'd better be careful about what?" Mark asked from the doorway. He was wearing my Hendrix T-shirt, Jimi gazing seriously from his chest. He had his own damp shirt bunched in one hand.

"About me," Sheila answered placidly, turning toward him. Her hands were on her hips, her chin high.

Mark snorted through his nose. "I'd agree," he said. "I'd agree with that fucking totally."

The profanity sounded far too loud, especially in my house with my Mom in the next room. But in Mark's gaze was the same heat that had been in his face as he'd brandished the headless body of Kitty-Kitty back in the woods. It was a dangerous enough look that I didn't even try to chastise him.

CHAPTER FOUR

The morning after our "discovery" of Sheila, Dad left to go back to Pittsburgh—he'd be back on weekends but would be spending the rest of the weeks there. I went into the woods early in the morning, after I helped Dad load his suitcases into the rental Rambler and waved him off with Mom.

Morning was another time I loved, especially unusually cool summer days like this one. It had rained during the night and tendrils of fog rose from the dense blanket of leaves like the slow breath of the earth. The tree trunks, branches and leaves close to me were sharp and colorful, but further away the mist started to gray and mute the colors, until everything in the distance became hazy and insubstantial. Sound was altered, also. The fiery crunch of dry, ancient leaves under my sneakers was sharp and distinct, but the quick hammering of an unseen woodpecker a hundred yards away was muffled, all the bright edges blunted by the clouded air.

By afternoon, I knew, the day would be humid and oppressive, yet at this moment, I felt almost cold, with beads of dew fringing my hair. The morning matched my mood: I could see no further or clearer into my own immediate future than I could glimpse the bottom of the valley ahead of me.

I heard the sound long before I could identify it: ...*doom*... ... *doom*... ...*doom*... A rhythmic, low pounding, like the beating of some gigantic heart. For a moment, I slipped into fantasy. I could imagine a dragon with an armored tail curled around a huge oak, the sound of its heated blood pulsing and sending out a call, a summons that only the true initiate could hear—and, of course, I was that unique individual, the one destined to be the dragon-rider. If I'd wanted, I could have followed that image, could have reached for the silver-bladed sword that hung at my side and pulled up the cowl of silken chain mail around my head, moving quietly through the enchanted forest of the Mullinswood, with its half-alive trees and strange creatures that slithered in emerald shadows below. I would go to meet the summons, to confront the waiting dragon or hear the geas the creature would lay upon me before it would let me approach to tame it...

But I shook my head, and I was dressed in jeans and T-shirt, and my fantasies—for the moment, anyway—were too adult to sustain a dragon. *...doom... ...doom... ...doom...* The sound came from across the ravine, toward South Crest. I half-slid down the hill in an avalanche of wet leaves, crossed the creek, and started up the other side, the sound growing more distinct and higher-pitched as I approached. Wood striking wood, the beat as steady as a metronome.

I saw her as I neared the top of the ridge, where the South Crest kids had made a trail from the dead-end street into the woods, along the spine of the hill and then down, meandering and occasionally narrowing almost to nothing, until you reached Cooper Creek maybe a half-mile in. Sheila was crouched off the trail, staring into the foggy recesses of the forest; I was behind her, looking at the generous fall of black hair over her back, at—yes, I'll admit it—the way her rear filled the fabric of her jeans. She had a branch or something in her hand, and was thumping a fallen, hollow log. As I drew closer, I could hear her singing in a soft voice, though the words seemed to be in some language I'd never heard before. I tried to get closer to listen better, but as I started to move, the stick in her hand stopped in mid-stroke.

"It's really not polite to sneak up on people," she said. Her head craned around over her shoulder, looking at me. "And you should also not be looking at my ass that way."

I could feel the heat flare on my cheeks. "I wasn't," I stammered.

"You weren't, eh...So my ass isn't worth looking at?"

I could feel my mouth hanging open as words jammed up at the entrance to my throat. "Umm, well, yeah, it is…" I stopped. That seemed the wrong thing to say, but I was trapped now. I decided just shutting up would be the best tactic.

"Why are *you* here, Rob?" she asked. "I really thought it would be Mark." She cocked her head at me, confusing me further. I didn't know what she wanted me to say. I had the sense of being caught in a game whose rules I didn't know.

"Mark? I don't know where he is. I didn't go over to his house…" I stopped, wondering why I hadn't gone to Mark's house first. Sheila was still watching me. I lifted my shoulders. "I mean, I heard you drumming on the log, and singing, and I thought I'd see who it was, and…"

"It's all right. It's not a question I expected you to be able to answer. It was more a question for me." She was laughing at me as she stood up. I could see the stick in her hand now—it wasn't a branch she'd picked up from the ground, but a length of polished wood, naturally knobbed at one end, with a wide carved band of intricate knotted lines just under the knob. If it was a walking stick, it was well-used one; I could see the discoloration and sheen around the flared end where hands had held it many times. The wood had that rich, dark umber that comes only with age. "What were you singing?" I asked her.

"A song my mom taught me. The words call the spirits of the dead for protection. You can see the spirits on mornings like this." She waved a hand to encompass the foggy landscape. "All the wisps coming from the ground, curling and dancing: that's them, rising up to greet the sun and drift in the clouds for a time before falling back to the ground as rain and sinking back to sleep. You really don't want to walk through them without protection—they get angry when you disturb them and they give you bad luck. You're lucky I was singing to them."

I nodded my head as if I understood without understanding at all. I didn't know if she was serious or if this was a game like those Mark and I used to play. But I was never going to know unless I asked. "It's an interesting fairy tale. Is it something from where your family came from or something you read in a book?"

Thick eyebrows lifted, thunderheads above twin, pale blue pools. A hand perched on hipbone. The stick tapped the ground. "It's the truth," she said. "You of all people should be able to feel that."

"Why me of all people? That's not a rational explanation."

She took a step toward me. The stick pounded into the ground an inch from my left foot with a loud *t-chunk*. "*I* believe it," she said. Her eyebrows had clambered high on her forehead. "You know why there are so many car wrecks on foggy days?"

"Umm, because people can't see very well?" I grinned.

"All those cars rushing through the dead souls and pushing them away get them irritated, and they place their curses on the drivers. That's why."

"Wow." I shook my head, still grinning. "And I thought *I* had a great imagination."

"*You*," she retorted, "have too firm a grasp on what you insist is your concept of reality. I could show you how to think with *all* of your mind, Rob, not just part of it. If that's something you *want* to understand."

For the first time I realized that she might not be joking, and I didn't quite know how to respond. "Sure. You'd just better do it quick. You only have a few weeks." It was a stupid thing to say, immediately conjuring up all the sublimated anger and fear I'd been feeling ever since the trip to Pittsburgh. I knew it for a mistake even as the words came out. I scowled, hands going into pockets, pissed at myself for bringing up the subject again and my parents for doing this to me. Now that I'd said it, the impending move hung there in the air between us like the fog.

Sheila's face changed, watching mine. The eyebrows slid down, the smile evaporated, her eyes narrowed slightly. She took a step back, then turned completely, going back to the log. She struck it once with the walking stick. The *tunk* was dead and muffled, no longer the ringing, gong-like *doom* of a minute before. She stared out into the mist, or perhaps into a sea of dead souls.

"What language was that you were singing in?" I asked, mostly trying to pull the mood back even though I knew it was irrevocably gone. "German?"

"None you'd know, or believe in if you did," she answered. She lifted the stick and let it fall again: *tunk*. "Come on, since it's you that showed up," she said. She let the walking stick fall down next to the log. I looked at it quizzically, wondering why she'd just abandon something as obviously old and ornate as that. "No one will bother it," she answered my unvoiced question. "They won't even see it. I'll pick it up on the way back. Come on."

She extended her hand toward me, palm up. There was invitation in the gesture, as if in responding I would be reaching across the first boundary between us—it wasn't a boundary I'd crossed all that much yet, and doing so was enough to make my breath come a little faster. She laced her fingers in mine as we stepped over the log, moving back toward the trail, but let my hand drop again a few moments later. I suppose she noticed my disappointment, because she laughed and took my hand in hers again. I squeezed her fingers slightly; she squeezed back. I knew we were saying something to each other, yet I didn't quite know what. "Where we going?" I asked.

"Does it matter? Do you need to go ask your parents first?" A grin. Her fingers threatened to release me again.

"No," I answered hurriedly.

"Then come on." With that, she started walking quickly down the path, pulling me with her. I went. I wanted to hold that hand forever.

We followed the trail all the way down to Cooper Creek. By the time we reached the bank, the sun was peeking over the tops of the trees and most of the fog had burned off. Cooper Creek was a sequence of small deep and slow pools connected by lengths where the water flowed quickly over flat stones. In the shallows, minnows flashed their silver flanks, darting in startled unison and retreating to deeper water as our shadows moved over them. Sheila crouched down at the edge of the creek, watching them. I wandered the shore, turning over rocks near the water. Mark and I had hunted salamanders in that way every spring and summer. Locally, we had the common Redback, the green Duskies, and the larger (and much rarer) blue-black Slimy Salamander, horribly misnamed as it wasn't slimy at all—the Slimy Salamander, with its bowlegged stance and bulbous eyes, always reminded me of a creature that might be used in a bad monster movie, a dinosaur's spinal frill glued to its back as it stomped through a miniature film landscape. I thought I'd find one of them to show Sheila. I flipped one particularly large rock, and saw a dark form flitter underneath. My next move was particularly stupid. I reached for the movement, instinctively. A moment later, I let the rock drop back, shaking my hand. "Ow! Shit!"

"What?"

"Snake. The damn thing bit me." I could see beads of red welling from a curved row of puncture wounds. "Shit!" My finger throbbed; the bite had hurt. I was feeling slightly panicked, imagining that my hand was already feeling numb. Mark and I had caught our share of snakes before; I'd been bitten a few times, naturally enough, but I'd always known that it was one of the numerous non-poisonous species before it happened and the bites had never hurt quite as much as this one. It had been years since anyone had reported seeing a copperhead, rattlesnake or cottonmouth in the area, as according to all the nature guides I'd collected over the years, Cincinnati was near the extreme northern edge of their range, but still...

I hadn't seen anything beyond a momentary glimpse of the snake that had just bitten me; I hadn't seen the coloring or the head shape, but I knew the damn thing had been bigger than most of the snakes I'd caught before. I also knew that poisonous snakes usually have large triangular heads; in my mind, the flash I'd seen of the snake had a huge head with prominent jaws. I stared at the marks on my hand, imagining the poison already swelling it, the muscle tissue beginning to dissolve under the attack of the powerful enzymes in the venom....

Sheila had already gone over to the rock, lifting it. "Careful," I said, cradling my hand. "The snake's already scared. Don't get yourself bit. Just see what it is."

I don't know if she heard me or not. "Sheila!" I called warningly, as she stretched her hand down casually, palm up. I thought I heard her whisper something. She came up with the green-striped length of the snake curling around her hand and arm—a large one, two feet long and as thick as my thumb. Its head lifted, rounded and small, the red tongue slithering in and out.

"Garter snake," she said, and the tingling in my hand eased as I saw the snake. "It's harmless. Just as frightened as you were."

"Didn't it bite you? You just reached down…" Sheila might not think so, but I *knew* snakes—Mark and I caught a dozen or more of them a year, usually keeping them in a bucket for a few days before letting them go again. This was easily the largest garter snake I'd seen—they were generally a foot or less in length. You can hold garter snakes easily and safely enough once they're used to being handled, which generally takes a day or so—but they always, *always* try to bite at first. Yet this one was winding contentedly around her hand as if it had been around her for months.

"I told her I wasn't going to hurt her," She grinned at me, holding the snake up so she could look at its face. "Didn't I, dear?" she said to it, crooning the words. Its tongue slithered in and out, tasting the air right in front of Sheila's own nose. She put her hand down on the ground, and the garter snake uncoiled itself from her arm and slid into the brush. "She's an old one, with a dozen clutches behind her. Now…Let me see your finger," Sheila said.

I held up my finger for her inspection. "Ouch," she said sympathetically. "She got you good, didn't she? Wait a second…" She let go of my finger and walked around the area, bending over and looking at the bushes and weeds at the creek's edge. She gave a cry of satisfaction and bent over, plucking a few leaves from a feathery plant winding around a sapling. "Here…" She crushed the leaves in her hand, dipped a little water into her hand from the creek to make a paste of the crushed leaves, and then started to take my injured hand. I pulled it away.

"What is that stuff?"

"Just trust me," she said. Her head cocked to one side, and her eyes looked at me challengingly. "Or not."

I suddenly had the sense that if I chose "or not," everything between us would change. I'd known her now for less than a full day, yet I already didn't want to lose her or do anything to push her away. I'd thought of that face and that smile all night. (I'd thought of other parts of her as well, and at least imagined what they might look like, but that's probably best left alone…) Shaking her head, Sheila placed the leaf-paste on the puncture wounds, smearing the blood. The stinging and throbbing started to slowly recede.

"Hey," I said. "That really works."

"Yeah," she said. "Duh."

"How'd you know to do that?"

"There's all kinds of learning in the world. There's the stuff we get in school, then there's the rest." She shrugged. "My mom taught me this. She knows all kind of remedies, plants that are growing out here that nobody thinks about, not anymore. She knows lots of interesting stuff, actually, and she's teaching me." She crushed the leaves a bit more in the palm of her hand, rubbing them around with her forefinger, then applied the goo to my finger. "Hold that on there for a few minutes," she said. "Then you can get rid of it."

We were very close, our hands still touching. At that moment, I wanted more than anything to kiss her. Our eyes held each other's gaze for what seemed like minutes but what I'm sure were only a few seconds. Her face seemed very serious and very sensual, and I leaned forward. I wasn't much experienced with girls—I'd exchanged a few quick pecks with a few girlfriends, but my first extended kissing and (very) minor fondling session had been just this April, with Debbie Berkley, who lived up on Crestmount Avenue. I seemed to be a bit behind most of the other boys my age in that department—assuming I could trust the stories my classmates told of their conquests. Debbie and I had spent a few furtive hours cuddled together on the swing on her back porch, me always half-lost in the heat that emanated from her mouth into the utter core of my body, and half-tensed for fear that her parents, or (worse) her older brother who was a senior at my school, would open the back door and catch us clenched together. We'd lasted three weeks, and then suddenly Debbie stopped talking when I called her, and I stopped going over. But for that short time, there had been a heat and passion in the relationship that was a new experience for me—and one I repeated in my mind many times at night.

I could feel the echo of that intensity now. I imagined what Sheila's lips would feel like under mine (exactly like Debbie Berkley's, that being the only example I had), wondered whether she would part her lips slightly as Debbie had done, letting our tongues touch and explore…

"I would have thought you'd have learned today not to reach for something you're not sure about."

The words were whispered, but very loud in our closeness. "Huh?" I said, dumped irreverently and suddenly out of fantasy. I'd closed my eyes in preparation for the kiss; I opened them. Her pale eyes glimmered a few inches away, unblinking. Her mouth was shut, drawn upward in a tight smile. I took a half-step away from her, as if trying to pretend nothing had happened. "What do you mean?"

"Sometimes when you move too fast, you get bit." Eyes sparkled. She tossed her dark hair away from her face, and made an exaggerated snapping motion with her teeth. I could hear the sinister *click*. "Gotta watch for those nasty snakes until you know what they are and what they might do to you."

I blinked.

"Why don't we head back to your house?" she said. "I took the sting away, but you still ought to put something on that bite to make sure it doesn't get infected. You should use a remedy *you* can believe in. Using what you believe in always works better."

Mark was at my house by the time we returned, his hand lifted to knock on the front door. He watched us as we emerged from the woods, an odd expression on his face. "Hey, where you two been?"

"Cooper Creek," I told him. "Got bit by a garter snake." I held my finger up for him. Mark looked at the row of teeth marks, barely red now, and sniffed.

"That was stupid," he said. His gaze slid across me to Sheila. "I never get bit. I'm too fast."

"I'll just bet you are," she told him. Mark grinned. The bruise on his left cheek had faded overnight, but he touched it, unconsciously grimacing as he did. "We came back to put some antiseptic on the bite."

Mark nodded, but to me rather than Sheila. "Go on and do what you need to do," he told me. I couldn't read his gaze. "We'll wait out here for you."

"Okay," I told them. "I'll just be a minute…"

It wasn't. My Mom caught me as I came in the door, asking where I'd been. By the time I'd talked with her, foraged through the disarray in the bathroom medicine cabinet and found the antiseptic, then uncovered the Band-Aids snuggled under the bath towels in the closet, it was more fifteen minutes than one.

When I came back out, they were gone.

"Mark!" I shouted. "Sheila!" There was no answer. I looked up and down the street, but the only person I saw was Mr. Bell cutting his grass; he saw me at the same time and shut off the mower, gesturing to me. I waved back, but he swept his hand through the air again, more emphatically. "You come here, boy," he called out. "I got a question for you."

I walked over to him reluctantly. Mr. Bell must have been a huge man in his time. He was still tall—six foot three even though his spine was bent and stooped over, and his shoulders, though bowed now with age, were still wide. He had liver spots all over his balding scalp and arms, and his eyes were a cloudy, filmy blue. He leaned over kids like a glowering thunderhead. He mopped at his face with a large blue handkerchief and stuffed it into the back pocket of his trousers. "Kitty-Kitty is missing," he said abruptly as I stopped at the low hedge that separated our yard from his.

I could feel the heat of my face as I looked up at him. He glared down at me accusingly, but then Mr. Bell always glared—it was one the few expressions he seemed to have in his repertoire. I told myself it didn't mean anything since after all, *I* hadn't snatched Kitty-Kitty and killed her; the deed had already been done when I found Mark. My rationalizing didn't do much about the guilt, and I wondered if Mr. Bell could see the warmth I felt on my cheeks and forehead. "Really?" I asked as innocently as I could. "That's too bad." I rubbed at my hands as if the bloodstains were still there, and I remembered how the headless body of the dachshund had curled into the shallow hole I'd dug for it with a flat stone, and how I'd rolled the head into the hole—putting it with a branch like a golf ball—because I didn't want to touch it...

"I wondered if you'd seen her," he said. "I asked that boy if he'd seen her, but he wouldn't answer me. He's going to be a juvenile delinquent, that boy; you mark my words." "That boy" had to be Mark, I knew. "So, have *you* seen Kitty-Kitty?"

I shook my head vigorously, as if I could make it true with emphasis. "I haven't seen her," I told Mr. Bell, "but I'll keep an eye out for her. She probably just saw a squirrel or something and went after it."

"She wouldn't have run away. Not by herself." He was still staring at me, as if he didn't quite believe me, and the lower lids of his eyes were wet. I wondered if he'd been crying, but that image contradicted everything I thought I knew about Mr. Bell. He grunted and cleared his throat. "You tell me if you find her, boy," he said finally. "If someone's hurt her, I'll..." He didn't finish the threat. He turned abruptly and went back to the mower. He yanked viciously on the starter cord, still staring at me. I waved at him and retreated.

I found myself angry again at Mark: for having gotten me involved in the sacrifice of Kitty-Kitty, for the way he'd reacted to me leaving, and more immediately for having taken off with Sheila without waiting for me. Mark wouldn't have taken Sheila to his house—he spent as much time as he could at mine, avoiding the squabbles and fights of his own family. I doubted they'd have gone to Sheila's.

No, they'd gone back into the woods.

I stood there on my front lawn, feeling betrayed and pissed off and abandoned, as well as irritated (and surprised) that Sheila would agree to go with Mark.

I could go into the woods looking for them, but there were a hundred ways they could have gone; knowing Mark, I figured he wouldn't take her to the obvious places where I could easily find them. Chances are I wouldn't find them and I'd just waste the day trying. I turned to go back into the house, figuring I'd read a book or watch TV and wait until they came back for lunch. I scuffed at the grass. A slip of paper lay on the trimmed blades a few feet in front of me, obvious enough that I wondered how I'd missed it when I'd come out of the house. I could see writing on it, and bent down to pick it up. The handwriting, in pale blue ink, was small and neat: definitely not Mark's. *Come to the gateway*, it said.

I thrust the paper in my pants pockets and headed into the woods toward the Seven Caves.

I heard them before I actually saw them, back in the vine-snared grove where Mark had discovered the stones, where he'd performed his bloody ritual with Kitty-Kitty the day before. "…why you'd care about that little asshole anyway. He's gone in a few weeks." Mark's voice. So it seemed I'd become an "asshole" in Mark's eyes…

Just to my left, I heard a soft patter like dirt being shoveled aside from a hole…and a voice. "Of *course* you've become an asshole," the voice said to me, and I looked over to see Kitty-Kitty standing atop the flat stones I'd laid over her shallow grave, staring up at me with cataract-white eyes. "You've told him you're out of his life, and yet you're still here," the dachshund continued. She sounded like someone's doddering grandmother, with a quavering voice. Her elongated body was smeared with blood and bits of dead leaves had stuck to her graying fur. "Worse, you're standing between him and Sheila." The head wobbled like that of a dashboard dog, as if poorly reattached. I stared. "I really should have bit him harder," Kitty-Kitty added.

"I'm sorry he did that to you," I told the dog, and she gave a small *yip* that sounded almost amused.

"No, you're not really. I bit you too, more than once. How many times did you think 'I'd like to kill that little bitch'?" She yipped again. "Sometimes, if you want something enough, you make it happen."

"I didn't—" I began to protest, then glanced away from the body to the grove where I could still hear Mark and Sheila talking. When I glanced back again, the stones over Kitty-Kitty's grave were unoccupied. I shivered.

"Maybe. Maybe not," I could hear Sheila saying to Mark. "Lots of things can happen in a few weeks. Whole *lives* can change in a few weeks, Mark, if you want them to."

"I think you've changed mine." There was a tone in Mark's voice I'd never heard before, though I'd hear it again in other voices in other times, including my own: the low, silken delivery of attempted seduction. Mark's words might have been clumsy and trite, but the intent was clear and it set off alarm bells in my ego.

"Hey!" I called out, glancing once more at Kitty-Kitty's grave before striding noisily into the grove. Mark's head turned toward me savagely; Sheila gave me a smile that I interpreted as relief. "You guys took off without me."

"We thought you weren't coming back out," Mark said. His body language said something else entirely, and his next words revealed the lie. "How the hell did you find us?"

"Sheila's note," I said. I pulled the paper from my pocket.

"She didn't leave a note. I'd have seen that." Mark snatched the paper from my hand, glanced at it, then looked at Sheila.

"Magic," she said, grinning.

That evening, Sheila invited us to dinner at her house. She lived at the utter end of South Crest where the street dead-ended at the edge of the woods. In fact, I hadn't realized there was even a lot there—Mark and I rarely went in or out of the woods via South Crest, and even though the street was just through my backyard and that of the house behind us, I didn't know South Crest all that well. The few school friends I had on that street all lived at the top end, not at the woods' end. Sheila's house was tiny, even by the standards of our suburb: one story, and it didn't look like the entire house was much bigger than the addition my parents had added to our place. No garage. No car in the driveway, either; I wondered how Sheila and her mom got to the grocery or went shopping; it was a good two-mile walk down to Reading Road and the bus line, downhill on the way in, but it would be a brutal uphill climb on the way back, laden with bags.

One of the guys in my class had once said to me, half-jokingly, "Hey, if you want to know what your girlfriend's gonna look like in twenty years, just check out her mom." If there was any truth to that at all, Sheila would be hardly changed in a few decades. Her mother *was* Sheila, grown: a few inches taller, maybe ten pounds heavier, fuller and mature, but with the same long black hair and pale blue eyes, the same too-wide mouth and nose. She wore a gauzy broomstick skirt, a loose blouse with floral patterns, and more and stranger jewelry than any other of the moms I'd ever seen, most of whom gravitated to pedal-pusher pants and tight-fitting blouses around the house. Bracelets clashed musically on her wrists; necklaces swayed as she opened the door. She looked like a pulp magazine's version of a gypsy. "Ah, so *you're* the ones Sheila's been talking about," she said. "Come on in."

I expected to see an interior decorated like the hippie apartments in the Haight I'd seen in magazines: crystals, candles, red scarves draped over lamps, incense burning in an ornate holder on a coffee table made from an old crate, that sort of thing. There was music wafting out from behind Sheila's mother, but the song was like nothing I'd ever heard before: airy, ethereal vocals against an insistent drum beat and some strange instruments that sounded nothing like the guitars, pianos or organs that I knew. The room we entered…it was almost Japanese in its simplicity, with white walls trimmed with thin, black-stained wood, and very little decoration other than a few chairs and a single table. The scene had an odd feeling of familiarity to me, though I couldn't quite decide why. The smell of something cooking wafted in from the kitchen.

"Shoes go over there," Sheila's mom—Mrs. Niemann, I assumed—said, pointing to a wooden rack to one side of the door. Mark and I looked at each other, but we took our shoes off while she went to the archway leading out into a tiny hallway. "Sheila!" she called. "Your friends are here." She glanced back at us. "Make yourselves comfortable," she said. "I need to check dinner."

Mark shrugged at me. "This is fucking weird," he whispered to me, and I nodded in agreement. I padded around the living room in my socks, wishing they were cleaner, and examining the items on display. I had to admit that the severity of the room heightened the impact of each piece; my parents (and me, in my room) had stuff crowded on every available flat surface and all over the walls, so much to look at that sometimes you just ended up ignoring the clutter entirely. You couldn't miss anything here: a single painting screamed against the sterile white walls, a black sweeping stroke on white paper, matted on gray; a dark vase with a crackled white glaze throbbed on the otherwise empty table between the chairs; a plant arrangement of two exotic flowers I couldn't name loomed atop the oak-and-tinted-glass case that held the stereo equipment.

"You like it?" Sheila asked as I leaned close to the painting, frowning.

I could see brush marks on the translucent paper. "Is that original?"

"Yes. My mother's work."

"It's nice," I said politely. I was thinking that if I took one of Dad's old paintbrushes and a can of black paint, I could do the same thing in about, oh, fifteen seconds. Mark was less circumspect; he snorted in amusement at my comment.

"It's zen calligraphy," Sheila said with a severe glance at Mark. "You spend a lot of time meditating and contemplating the stroke you want to make, you gather up the energy and at the right moment you do it all at once. In about"—there was a distinct pause—"oh, fifteen seconds."

That bit of serendipity, uttered in nearly the same tone I'd used in my reverie, turned my head, but she wasn't looking at me. She'd gone over to Mark, who was crouched in front of the stereo. There were several unfamiliar pieces of equipment in the case, but there didn't seem to be a turntable; I wondered where it was hidden. "We can put on something else if you want."

"Nah, that's all right." He shook his head, standing up. In the room, he looked clumsy and uncomfortable, too big and physical for the environment. "This place is bizarre," he declared.

"You don't like bizarre? That's a shame. I've always thought a house couldn't help but reflect the people who lived in it." I could hear the teasing in her voice, and Mark's face reddened.

"Hey, I didn't mean—" he started, then stopped himself. I was glad to see that Sheila could fluster him the same way she did me. His cheeks were turning red, and he was trying to find something to say in return before Sheila's mom rescued him by coming back into the room, carrying a lacquer tray.

"Supper's on the table," she said. "If you don't mind, I'm going to eat in my room; the kitchen's so small, you'll be more comfortable that way." Her smile was identical to Sheila's, with the same asymmetry.

"Thanks, Elisa," Sheila said. Mark and I looked at each other.

"Elisa?" I asked as we sat down at the table in the kitchen, which was indeed small. "You call your mom Elisa?"

"Sure. That's her name."

"Maybe when I get back I'll say 'Hey Donna, I'm home' and count how many seconds until Mom explodes and then grounds me for the next decade," I told her. "I don't think I'll make it to three. What do you call your Dad: Fred? Tom?"

She just looked at me blandly. "I don't have a Dad," she said. That left me with my mouth hanging open, not knowing what I should say next. Mark saved me.

"My dad would kill me if I called him 'Jason,'" Mark said. "Literally."

"I believe that," Sheila responded somberly. Any residue of my jesting tone evaporated in that instant. She was looking at the fading bruise on Mark's face. Mark realized it and touched his face. "I'm sorry for you," she said to him.

Mark's face had flushed again, but from a darker emotion than embarrassment this time. "He won't do it again," Mark said. "Next time, I won't let him."

Sheila flicked a glance over at me. "I know," she said, very softly and quietly. "I know you won't."

Neither one of us believed that. Probably, Mark didn't either.

Sheila reached to the bamboo mat in the middle of the table and passed me a bowl of rice, I took a scoop and handed it to Mark, and then ladled some of the stir-fried vegetables on top. Sheila gave me a pottery bowl holding fried white cubes. "What's this?"

"Tofu," she said. "Bean curd."

The stuff shook like opaque jello. I glanced at the bowls on the table and realized there was no meat to be had. That seemed to fit. I figured I'd be fixing a burger when I got home. "Tofu," I repeated. "It sounds like a sneeze, and it looks like snot."

Sheila looked at me with eyebrows arched into thunderheads. "Eat it and shut up," she said. "I asked the two of you over here so I could get to know you better. And that includes seeing how you react to things you're not used to."

I shut up. I ate it.

* * *

As it turned out, I did fix that burger—the tofu tasted just fine, though I wasn't about to make a steady diet of the stuff. But by the time I got home, I felt famished, as if I hadn't eaten at all. My dad always used to joke about Chinese food: "You eat it and an hour later you're hungry again." My Mom asked the usual questions: about dinner (I think she took a subtle pleasure in the fact that I was frying a burger at the time); about Sheila's house; about her family. I gave her the usual one-syllable replies in return, and eventually she got tired of prying information from me one nugget at a time and wandered off to watch television.

I went to the bathroom. As I sat down on the commode, I saw the array of magazines in the holder alongside, and it all clicked. Most of the magazines were my mother's, and sometimes for lack of anything else to read while I was doing my business, I'd leaf through them. I rummaged through the rack until I found the one I wanted: the August issue of *Better Homes and Gardens*. I flipped the pages, looking for the article I dimly remembered from a few days ago. The headline "The Japanese Aesthetic" registered after I'd gone a few pages past it, and I went back. There, under the headline, was a photo of an interior: white walls, black wood trim, sparse furniture.

It was, as nearly as I could tell, an exact replica of what I had seen in the living room of Sheila's house. I scanned the caption under the photo, wondering if the magazine could possibly have sent the photographer to the house on South Crest, but the picture was credited to a house in San Francisco, and the family wasn't the Niemanns.

I held the magazine on my lap, staring at the photo, at the room I'd been in only a few hours before. Mrs. Niemann must have seen this same article, must have fashioned her living room after it.

"Weird," I muttered.

CHAPTER FIVE

I went over to Mark's house the next morning after driving down to the UDF to get some milk for Mom. When I knocked on the door, his little sister Jackie answered, opening the front door and peering up at me through the rusty, partially-torn screen of the storm door. "He can't come out," she said before I had a chance to ask for Mark.

"Why not?" It was a question I'd ask Jackie, but never her parents. Mrs. Dyson would just look scared and frightened at being "interrogated." JD would probably come right through the screen and throttle me for my impertinence.

"He just…can't," she answered, with a hesitation on the last word and a strange look of satisfaction on her face before she closed the door with finality. I thought for a second about knocking again, but I heard JD's voice, muffled but still loud and evidently near the door, and decided against the idea. Instead, I wandered around the back of their house, went into the backyard and looked up at the second-floor window that was Mark's bedroom, just in case, but the window was dark and empty. I jogged to the rear of the yard and hopped the fence into the small field that was the buffer between the manicured grass and the trees. I glanced back once at the house and thought I saw Mark at his window. I waved; a hand waved back.

I figured Mark was grounded for something; my parents threatened me with that occasionally though they'd yet to ever follow through. I went into the woods.

Under the trees, the summer heat seemed cooler and more humid. Under the trees, I could pretend that there was no "For Sale" sign planted in my lawn. Under the trees, there were no restrictions of time or place or reality…at least until it was time to go home for lunch.

After supper last night, the three of us had agreed to meet at Seven Caves in the morning, back at the gateway. I'll admit that part of me was just as glad that Mark wouldn't be there.

"Hey," I heard Sheila say as I approached. "Where's Mark?"

"Grounded or something," I told her. "At least that's what Jackie said. His dad's home too, which is weird. I wonder if he got canned."

Sheila looked wonderful to me: tight-legged, bell-bottomed jeans, loose T-shirt tucked into the waistband, sitting with her legs folded underneath in front of the twin pillars of cut granite. A cone of sunlight slashed down through the leaves, pollen glinting around her as the specks drifted into the light. She had one hand placed on the front of the left column, with specks of embedded mica and quartz flaring through her fingers. The sunlight struck her black hair and died, absorbed; her light eyes seemed more blue than usual, her teeth flashed as she smiled.

"What are you doing?" I asked.

"Just…feeling," she said. "Here, put your hand on this…"

I knelt down, dead leaves crunching under me, next to her. She took my hand, placing it on the rectangular blocks of stone. I almost lifted my hand away again in reflex as I touched the rock. "It's hot," I said.

"Uh-huh," she said. Her hand was still on top of mine, pressing it to the stone.

"It's in the sun," I said, searching for a reasonable explanation for the heat that was radiating out from the granite block.

She lifted my hand, placed it on another rock, a common lump of shale. If anything, it felt as cool as the moss on which it sat. "That's in the sun, too," she said.

"Yeah, but maybe it was in your shadow, or we just knocked away the leaves that were covering it."

She let go of my hand then. We knelt facing each other. "Maybe Mark's right," she said.

"What do you mean?"

She shrugged. "He says you've lost your sense of wonder and your imagination. That you can't *see* things anymore."

"What does *that* mean?" I knew. Images of Mary Martin as Peter Pan rose in my mind. "*I can't fly, Peter,*" Wendy was saying. "*Not anymore. I'm old now...*"

Sheila was looking at me, nodding as if listening to my thoughts. "Most adults...well, they close off most of the doors. Things can only be one way. A stone is just a stone, and if you see a bunch of them put together like this"—she put her hand on the gateway column next to her—"it's just something some people put together. Nothing more." She paused. "Touch it," she said to me. "Go ahead. Touch it."

I hesitated a moment, then put my hand next to hers on the stones. They were cool. As cold as stone should be. I could feel my eyebrows squinting suspiciously as Sheila watched me. I could also feel the heat of her hand next to mine. I placed my hand on top of hers. She didn't move. Her eyes searched mine, her lips parting slightly. I felt like I was falling into her, as if I were a satellite pulled into the gravity of her world. "Sheila, I—" I stopped.

"I didn't believe Mark," she told me. "I knew he was just saying that because he didn't want me to be interested in you. He wants me to be interested in him."

I couldn't stop myself from asking the question. "So are you?"

Her mouth slid into frown and she looked away, and I felt like a fist had just slammed into my stomach. I cursed at myself for making her give me the answer. *Asshole...*Then she glanced back, her lips arcing in a smile. "He was the one I heard first," she said. "But somehow, right or wrong, you have the stronger voice for me."

There are moments in your life when the world suddenly comes into sharp, intense focus, when the sun is brighter, the colors more saturated, the sounds crisp and brilliant, the taste and feel of life so rich that you're almost overwhelmed. For me, one of those moments was hearing those words. I could feel my face pulling into a helpless grin, and I wanted to laugh and shout.

But self-denial's a part of every good Catholic kid's upbringing, too...

"Sheila, I've gotta be straight with you. You know I'm leaving. By the time the summer's over…"

"Maybe. Maybe you're leaving."

I shook my head. "There's no 'maybe,'" I told her. "My dad's leaving for Pittsburgh later this afternoon and staying up there. We bought a house there, I'm registered for school, Mom's already given notice at her job. It's done."

"Maybe," she still insisted. "You need to choose what your heart wants most. Do you know what that is, Rob? Do you know what you want?"

I was looking at her. "Yeah," I told her. "I do." I leaned forward, closing my eyes. I could feel my heart pounding, the blood rushing in my temples and pulsing like audible heat in my ears. I thought that she would stop me, as she'd done the last time I tried to kiss her.

She didn't.

Her lips were impossibly soft and yielding. Velvet and silk., and so warm. I could have stayed there, trapped willingly forever.

Something moved in the underbrush behind us. We both moved back. I hurtled to my feet with a guilty outrush of breath but Sheila just sighed, as if she hadn't been startled at all, as if she'd expected this. Something—someone—went crashing through the foliage, thrashing wildly away from us. I caught a glimpse of white cloth through the vines, of brown hair, of a back I knew all too well from following it through the woods so many years. "Shit!" I said.

I realized that we were still holding hands. Her fingers pressed against mine. "Mark," she said. It was not a question. I nodded.

"Hell," I said. "Goddamn it." I didn't even notice that I was cursing. I wanted to run after him; I wanted to stay. I listened to the fading sounds of his wild retreat, then glanced at Sheila. She was staring into the woods, her face stricken. Her hand let go of mine.

"Go after him," she said. "He'll need you."

"You're the one he wants," I told her. "Not me."

"Not now. I'm the one who betrayed him," she said. "I've evidently made my own choice." She shivered, hugging herself in the heat. "Go on," she told me again. "Go on and find him."

* * *

In the woods, Mark could run like a deer, slipping easily and quickly between trees, bounding over tree trunks and slipping down hollows, unerringly finding the best path while I blundered and struggled behind him. It wasn't any different now. By the time I started after him, he was already out of sight and gone. It took me a good fifteen minutes to come out of the woods into the back-yards of North Crest, then run up the street toward Mark's house.

When I got there, out of breath and panting, I ran up the steps and started to knock. Stopped. Inside, I could hear loud voices.

"...the fuck were you thinking? You were grounded, and now I find out that you snuck out of the damn house!"

"You don't understand, Dad! Just shut up and listen a minute!"

I could hear the sound of the slap, the crisp smack of a hand against a cheek. I could nearly see Mark's head snap to one side with the blow, his skin turning bright red where he'd been struck, the scared fury rising in his eyes. "You don't tell *me* to shut up!" JD screeched. I heard another slap. "Goddamn it, boy! You *look* at me when I'm talking to you! Look at me!"

"Dad..." I could hear the break of a sob in Mark's voice. Then I heard him gasp, as if his father had pulled him around by the ear or caught his chin in a hand.

"No! You listen! You're fucking grounded for good. No car, no TV, no hanging out with your stupid friends, nothing. You won't go out of your goddamn room until I decide to say so. You understand me?"

"Dad!"

This time the sound of the blow was meatier, thicker, and Mark grunted. I heard his mother give a short little scream: "JD! Stop it! Stop it, please!" and heard him bark back at her.

"You stay out of this if you know what's good for you, woman." I could feel the threat of violence under his words.

I backed away from the door, walking softly, quietly down the steps and then turning and running down the sidewalk to the street. Halfway between my house and Mark's, I stopped. I felt as if I wanted to throw up.

I've often thought back to that moment, and the choice I made then. It was, I think, one of those pivotal moments in my life, where I had to choose a path that I would be forced to follow for the rest of my time.

I should have gone to my parents. I should have told them what I'd heard, told them that JD was hitting Mark and threatening Mrs. Dyson; I should have called the police and reported the abuse. Times were different then, yes—there weren't the organizations and the awareness and the open talk that there is now. There were no mandatory reporting laws, no processes, no "9-1-1" calls. Parents used physical discipline with their kids, and wives sometimes covered up bruises with make-up and dark glasses, and no one would say much; I'd see it at least every other time I went to the grocery store. But still, I could have done something...*should* have done something.

Life is full of "should haves." Maybe each one leads to a different future. Maybe each decision we make creates a new fork in the road of our fate. I don't know. I do know that I'll always wonder about that one.

We only get to choose one path, and that one path is the only one we'll ever see; all the others instantly vanish except in our imagination. Regret is a useless emotion. That's what I kept telling myself, afterward.

I made the choice to do nothing at all.

I stood at the curb, staring back at Mark's house, imagining myself striding angrily back up to the front door and banging on it with a fist, shouting at JD that I knew what he was doing in there and he'd damn well better stop or I'd call the police or my parents, or even—in the most overt fantasy—barging in there myself and, with Mark's help, stopping JD from hitting anyone at all. Forever.

I thought of going to my parents, but by the time I told them and something happened, it would all be over anyway. I wouldn't have stopped the beating. I remembered the last time and how Mark had denied that his bruises were anything but an accident. He'd say the same thing again if we brought in the police, I told myself, and then God knows what JD would do to him afterward in retaliation. He'd hurt Mark worse than ever.

I was frozen, caught between fear of what would happen if I did intervene and what would happen if I didn't. I took the easier road: I didn't do anything.

Or rather, what I *did* do was go back into the woods to find Sheila.

I could see the fear and concern in Sheila's eyes, but she said what I wanted her to say. Somehow, it did nothing to ease the guilt I was feeling. "There wasn't anything you could do, Rob. If you had interfered, his dad would just have hurt Mark worse, and maybe he'd have hurt you, too. You were scared; I understand that."

"I wasn't scared," I spat defiantly. "You don't know that."

She shrugged and looked down at the ground. "Actually, yes I do," she said quietly. "That's what you were feeling, wasn't it?"

I could feel my eyes narrowing, wanting to deny it again but unable to lie into her stare. "Yeah, maybe, but it's just a goddamn excuse. *Fuck!*" I stamped my foot on the ground; it made an unsatisfying, dull thud, but at least the earth didn't open and swallow me for the profanity. "So what happens now?"

"I really don't know." Her voice sounded so strange, so distressed, that I looked over at her. She'd slumped down, sitting with her back to one of the gateway's columns. "I honestly don't know anymore. I did before. It was all so clear, but it's all changed now. It's my fault."

"What's changed? Why is any of this your fault?"

Her head lifted and she looked at me. She was crying now, twin tracks of moisture running down her cheeks. "Mark saw us," she said. "That shouldn't have happened. It wasn't supposed to happen. It *wouldn't* have happened if I hadn't...you hadn't..." Her shoulders lifted with a sob, and I sank down to my knees alongside her. I pulled her to me. For a moment, she resisted, then let me draw her into my arms.

"Sheila..."

Abruptly, she pushed me away, getting quickly to her feet. "I have to go," she said.

"Go? Where?"

She didn't answer. She shivered, hugging herself quickly, then ran through the gateway, moving not toward the houses but deeper into the woods. "Sheila!" I called after her, standing. "Hey!" She kept running. After a moment, I started after her.

Mark might move through the woods like a deer, leaping and gliding, but Sheila was a mist driven by a wild wind. I followed after her, calling her name, nearly sliding down the steep hill on the other side of the gateway in my rush. By the time I'd reached the bottom and crossed the small creek there, Sheila was already at the top of the next hill: I saw a glimpse of her white shirt as she topped the ridge and started down the other side. "Sheila, wait!" I called again. I climbed the hill, panting. When I reached the summit and looked down, I couldn't see her at all. There were only the trees, receding into an emerald gloom. I should have been able to see her or at the very least hear her from the top of the hill; she'd been at most fifty yards ahead of me. But there was nothing.

"Sheila!"

I could hear the faint echo of my voice, mocking. And then an answer: "I'm here, Rob." She was standing on the path at the foot of the hill. I blinked, certain she hadn't been there a moment before. "If you're going to follow me, then come on," she said. I went down to her, and she pushed through a screen of high weeds and onto a narrow, twisting path that—somehow—I'd never seen before in all the time I'd been prowling these woods. We walked, her hand in mine, for what seemed to be several minutes. I squinted up at the sun, suddenly confused as to what direction we were walking. Surely we must be coming out of the woods soon…the patch of trees that made up our woods wasn't *that* large…

"Here," Sheila said at last. "This is it."

We'd walked into a sloping, open glade. The nearly perfect circle of a field was hemmed in by a dozen straight, ancient trees. Their thick trunks went up a good thirty feet or more before the first branches started. Their crowns, a hundred feet above, nearly came together in a green roof. Spending as much time as I did in the woods, I was somewhat of an amateur naturalist; I had several field guides at home for trees, for reptiles and amphibians, for nature in general. They'd all once been on the big bookcase in the front room. I could identify most local trees on sight by the pattern of their leaves or the appearance of the bark, but I stared at these trees, puzzled. A sapling was growing in the shadow of the parent trees, and I plucked a small branch from it. The leaves were elongated, with a prominent sawtooth edging, the base of the blade tapering quickly in to the stem; turning it in my hands, I saw that the top and bottom were both nearly the same shade of green. There were large nut burrs on the branches above me as well, with fine, dense spines. All the trees around the glade were the same species.

I thought I could hear Cooper Creek nearby, but all the sounds of civilization seemed to be gone. "This is an interesting place," I said. "You know what kind of trees these are?"

"My mom called them sweetnuts. I'm sure that was a made-up name, though. Mom…she always said every tree had its own name for itself, and if you listened hard enough, it would tell you."

I shook my head. "I thought I knew all the places in the woods, but I've never been here before."

"I wouldn't let you come here before."

"You wouldn't *let* me?" She just stared at me, and I eventually just shook my head. "Okay, I'll bite. Why not?"

She gave a shrug, tossing her hair to one side at the same time. "This is where I was born," she said.

"Here?" I couldn't keep the incredulity and laughter out of my voice. "What, like this is where your life changed? This is where you come to think or meditate or something?"

She gazed at me with an eerie calm, her odd light blue eyes unblinking. "No. I mean literally. This is where I was born."

"Out *here*?" I searched for some reasonable explanation and found nothing. "Did your mom go walking this way when she was pregnant with you and suddenly go into labor?"

"No. This is where she lived."

I could feel my forehead creasing into long furrows. I scanned the field, looking for the tumbled ruins of a foundation, some sign that this place had once been occupied. I mean, Sheila was my age, so if she'd lived here even as a baby, there should have been the tumbled-down remnants of the house; even if it had burned down the day after she'd been born, there'd be *something*. But there was nothing, and the closeness of the old trees showed that there was never a road back here, not in the last several decades. "Where was your house, Sheila?" I asked.

"Here," she said. Her arms went wide, indicating the area around us. "Where it's always been. It's *still* here, but you can't see it, can you?"

"See what?" I was beginning to feel confused and a little concerned. Sheila's face and her voice were so absolutely serious. I wanted her to laugh and tell me it was a joke, that she was playing at a fantasy like Mark and I always had, but she didn't. Her gaze was entirely solemn, as if she expected me to understand. I didn't. I couldn't. "Sheila, I don't get what you're trying to tell me..."

"Stop talking, then," she told me. "Words are just going to push it further away." She faced away from me then, striding out to the very center of the circle. She stood there, her hands spread wide and her face lifted toward the emerald canopy above. Her eyes were closed but her mouth moved as if she were praying. I could hear faint words, but they didn't sound like English but the language I'd heard her chanting when she was drumming on the log.

I waited. With the heat of the day, and the long walk, I was tired enough that I sat down with my back to one of the trees. Sheila didn't move, didn't pay any attention to me. Nothing much seemed to be happening at all, so I closed my eyes. Sheila's incantations merged slowly into the sounds of birds and the rustling of leaves.

The form came slinking out of the darkness: Kitty-Kitty. The dachshund's fur was no longer blood-streaked, though her head still bobbed precariously on a few loose strands of fur and muscle. She didn't say anything this time, just barked once angrily at me. I thought she might dart forward and bite at my feet as she'd often done, but as Kitty-Kitty started toward me her body began to melt and change and grow, until by the time it reached me it was no longer Kitty-Kitty but a wolf whose shoulders would have come up to my hips. The great beast sat on its haunches in front of me. Wind ran unseen fingers through its gray fur as light blue and intelligent eyes regarded me. I stared back, calmly. It was snowing inside the ring of trees, though I wasn't cold. I could feel the warmth of the wolf's breath and see the faint clouds roll away from its mouth. A red tongue lolled in the nest of teeth.

"You're not the one who called her," the beast said in a hoarse, accented voice, and I smelled blood and old meat. Lacy snowflakes drifted through the air between us. "She should have been more careful. That was stupid on her part. Now she's afraid of what's going to happen."

"What will happen?" I asked. Oddly, it didn't seem strange to be having a conversation with a wolf.

The creature seemed to grin, and there was a hunger and violence in the expression. "Nothing good," it answered. For the first time, I felt a shiver of fear and it sniffed the air between us, as if tasting the emotion. "Excellent," it said. "That's the way you *should* feel."

It padded a slow step closer. The wind howled and the wolf lifted its head and howled with it: as the snow streaked past, half blinding me, the wind shifting so it drove the blizzard directly into my face. I brought my hands up, closing my eye against the cold sting of snow. The wolf's howl ended abruptly and I opened my eyes, expecting the creature to leap at my throat.

Only both wolf and winter were gone. Sheila was still in the same position, swaying as she stood with arms outstretched, and I saw tears tracking down the side of her face to fall into her dark hair. There was no wind, but the limbs above her swayed with her and a finger of sunlight caught her where she stood. She opened her eyes then and seemed to nod, even as the branches high above closed in again.

Sheila sat abruptly in the grass and plucked at the stalks in front of her, looking at the circle of trees. "What just...?" I started to ask her, still half-lost in wolf-dream.

"You go to church. I come here. You always believed these woods were magical, didn't you? Well, you're right." She looked at my face, and the smile she gave me was touched with the same kind of sadness I'd seen in Brother O'Leary's face in religion class when he talked about the poor heathens. "Mark was the same way when I tried to show him."

"You showed Mark this place? When?" I was suddenly jealous. "Sheila, look, you gotta admit this is all a little strange, you saying you were born here..." I looked around the circle and shivered; the place had an atmosphere, I had to admit that; I had the feeling that the trees were listening to me, and I could imagine wolves—or perhaps just the ghost of Kitty-Kitty—skulking beyond the ring. "You told us you'd just moved here to South Crest, but now you're saying..."

"There *is* no house on South Crest, Rob."

I laughed then, unable to help myself, and the sound was cold and harsh in this place, with no echo. When I stopped, it seemed like the trees had swallowed the sound. "I was *there*, Sheila, just yesterday."

"It was never there. I just made you think it was."

I blinked. She was so serious, so solemn. I stood there, my hands moving as if I were trying to speak, but I didn't have any words. "I know what you're thinking," Sheila said. "But I'm not crazy. Mark was the same. Even after I showed him, I don't think he really believed me. He found a way to convince himself that it was all a trick, that it was a dream or a hallucination or that I'd managed to hypnotize him somehow." She looked at me harshly. "He forced it out of his mind, and that's what you're probably going to do too."

"What," I asked, "are you talking about?"

Sheila nodded as if to herself. She brushed at her pants, then stood up. "Maybe I made another mistake," she said. "You can follow me out." She turned and started walking back the way we'd come, into the shadow of the trees.

"Sheila! Hey!"

"I wouldn't stay here," her voice came back, drifting through the earth-rich air. "This isn't a safe place at night for someone like you."

"What the heck is that supposed to mean?" I called back. "I'm not some little kid afraid of the dark..."

There was no answer. I thought I could hear a large animal moving through the underbrush just behind me and glanced behind, half-expecting to see a gray form. "Shit," I said, cringing a little as if someone—the trees, maybe, or dream-wolves, or Father Brautski—could overhear my profanity, then started after her. The path was empty, but I caught a glimpse of her far ahead, just rounding a bend. I ran after her. For several minutes, winding through the trees, I could see her momentarily, then she'd disappear again. Finally, I came around a small ridge and realized that I knew where I was again. "Sheila!" I called once more, but there was only the rustling of the wind in the treetops and the distant sound of cars in the subdivision several hundred yards away. I glanced back. The path seemed to have disappeared in the tangle of underbrush. The high weeds and thorns had come together again, and I couldn't see where we'd moved through them.

I realized that I was still holding the branch I'd pulled from the sapling in the glade. I clenched it tighter in my hand as I went forward into the familiar woods.

CHAPTER SIX

Mom wasn't home when I got back to the house. There was a note on the refrigerator door, something about having left to show a house, that she'd be back in a few hours, and to make myself whatever I wanted for lunch. I opened the refrigerator door and stared into the cool brightness, not even really seeing anything in there. All the hunger had been burnt out of me, and I was full of the words I'd wanted to say. Too much had happened already today: the kiss, Sheila's strange behavior in the woods, and Mark...

Mark. Guilt made my stomach burn all the way to the back of my mouth.

"Mom, listen: when I went over to Mark's, I heard him and his dad arguing, and...well...he was hitting Mark, Mom. I could hear it..." I could imagine her face going red with anger, and her picking up the phone and calling someone, the police, probably; I didn't know who. But I knew she'd do *something*.

But she wasn't here. And though I'd imagined telling Mom about Mark as I walked out of the woods, I wondered, even if she had been home, whether I really would have said anything. The honest answer was "probably not." Over the last several years, I'd been confiding in my parents less and less, until silence-unless-spoken-to was the normal *modus operandi*. Even my protests about the impending move had been weak and half-hearted. I never told them how deeply I resented it, how much I really wanted to stay *here* and that I didn't care if Dad never made any more money than he already did, that this was home and I had no interest in being torn away from everything and everyone I had here. I slammed shut the refrigerator door; jars and shelves inside crashed glassily with the movement. I picked up the kitchen phone and held it to my ear, listening to the dial tone with my fingernail hovering above the "0" hole in the rotary dial.

"Hello? This is Rob Mullins up on North Crest. I want to report a case of child abuse....No, I didn't actually see anything...Yes, but I could hear Mark and his dad arguing and I think I heard JD hit Mark...No, I can't say for certain that JD wasn't just slapping the wall or something; I told you, I didn't see the beating...No, he's not a little kid; he's sixteen...No, I don't think it's life threatening, but...No, the argument's over now...You can't send someone right now? Call if I hear anything again? Call while it's actually happening? But...

The phone was wailing in my ear. I pressed the receiver down and picked it up again, this time actually dialing "0." Sheila should be home by now; maybe she'd be willing to talk, maybe together we could decide what to do. "Operator, I need the phone number for 227 South Crest Drive. Niemann's the last name. They just moved in..." I waited, tapping my foot impatiently.

I heard a rustling of paper on the other side. "I'm sorry, sir, I don't have any listing at all for that address."

"Are you sure?"

The operator sounded slightly annoyed at that. "Yes, sir. I'm sure."

"Thanks," I mumbled. I hung up the phone. Picked it up again and dialed another number. If the wrong person had answered, I would have hung it up quickly. But it was Mrs. Dyson. "Hi, Mrs. Dyson. Umm, this is Rob. Can I, uh, talk to Mark?"

"I'm sorry, Rob, but Mark's been grounded. He's not allowed phone privileges right now." I listened carefully to the voice. She didn't sound different, didn't sound like she'd been crying or that she was upset, at least no more than usual. It was just mousy Mrs. Dyson with her quiet, breathy, timid voice, talking to me like it was any other day. I could hear Jackie in the background, laughing at something on the TV. The background of the house sounded entirely normal and peaceful.

"Umm, yeah. Sorry. Tell him…tell him I called, and to give me a call when he can, okay?"

"Sure, I'll do that, Rob." She hung up. I held the receiver to my ear until I heard the line click and the dial tone howled at me again. I hung up…and saw the leaf that I'd placed there in the wall phone's cubby when I'd walked in. I picked up the leaf.

By reflex, I went into the front room, but the wall that had once been dominated by a massive bookcase mocked me with its freshly-painted emptiness. Scowling, I trudged down to the basement to where Dad and I had stacked up the boxes of books. I prowled through them until I finally found my battered and old *Golden Guide to Trees*. I took the book back upstairs to my room and flipped through the pages, laying on my bed with the leaf alongside the book. The only leaf I found that looked like it might be the right one was a listing on the "Beech Family," where they showed a picture of an American Chestnut leaf. But there wasn't a listing in the book for the American Chestnut, just a note that "…this important forest tree was almost completely destroyed by a rampant fungus disease; only a few scattered sucker growths remain." I went to the basement again to find the set of encyclopedias Mom had bought a few years ago. There, under "Chestnut, American" was a large black-and-white picture: I knew it, immediately. I read the entry:

The American Chestnut: A deciduous tree (genus *Castanea*) of the Beech family, with thin-shelled, sweet, edible nuts encased in bristly burrs. The American Chestnut was once widely distributed in the Northern Hemisphere, ranging north to south from Maine to Florida, from the Piedmont west to the Ohio valley. The American Chestnut was a dependable and plentiful source of food for wildlife, and was prized for its straight-grained wood, which produced lumber as rot-resistant as redwood.

However, the American Chestnut is now sadly nearly extinct due to the chestnut blight (*Cryphonectria parasitica*), a bark fungus disease imported from Asia. The blight was first discovered in New York City in 1904 and spread very quickly, leaving behind in its wake dead and dying trees. By the middle 1930s, all stands of the American Chestnut were entirely gone. None of them remain now except for a very few single specimens, almost all of which show some signs of the blight.

Attempts have been made to create a blight-resistant tree by crossing the American Chestnut with resistant Chinese Chestnuts, but the efforts so far have yielded unsatisfactory results.

Chestnut Identification: American Chestnut leaves: elongated leaf with large, prominent sawtooth edges and a sharply tapering base. The underside of the leaf is a slightly lighter green where exposed to sun. Chinese Chestnut leaves: Oval shaped leaves with small teeth on edge. The base is rounded. The underside of the leaf is whitish and hairy.

I took up the twig with my leaf on it, twirling it in my fingers and looking back and forth from it to the encyclopedia. There was no doubt in my mind at all: my leaf was definitely the same leaf—American Chestnut, not Chinese. There were pictures of blight-savaged trees, yet none of the trees I'd seen had displayed any obvious signs of the blight. They were healthy and straight and huge.

And from what I had just read, they were also impossible. They shouldn't have been there. I stared at the leaf. It adamantly refused to go away.

I went out the back door and cut across the backyards to South Crest. Yes, the house was there, as I remembered it. No matter what Sheila had claimed in the woods, her house *was* there and the bricks felt solid and substantial and hurt my hand when I slapped them, stupidly, just to make sure. I rang the bell, listening to the chime ring. No one came to the door. After a few minutes, I opened the screen and knocked hard on the front door. No answer.

As I walked away from the small porch, I happened to glance up at the wires strung along the street. None of them ran from the nearest pole to Sheila's house. So the operator was right: there was no telephone service to the house, and apparently no electricity, either. I thought that was strange—after all, there'd been the stereo in the house and we'd heard it playing, and the doorbell had rung when I pressed it—but at the moment the only important thing was this meant that I didn't have a way to contact Sheila and ask if she had spoken with Mark.

Just another strangeness surrounding her.

I sat down on the front porch steps to wait. An hour later, Sheila still hadn't come back.

I told myself that it was a sign. If I'd been meant to do *something*, my Mom would have been home, or Mrs. Dyson would have sounded upset, or Sheila or her mom would have been there. God or the Fates or whomever was in control of the world would have made sure of that. Because He or They or It hadn't done so, I was absolved. I'd been *meant* to do nothing.

The answer didn't satisfy, though. I really wanted to talk with Sheila: about Mark, about us, about everything. I could think of the most likely place for her to be, and I figured that since I'd been there once, I could find the grove of chestnuts again easily enough.

I retraced my steps: back to the gateway and down the path to the bottom of the hill. Everything was familiar: the valley, the slope, the small creek bed, the thorny underbrush. The path to Sheila's grove was *here*. Or it should have been here, anyway. I walked along the path, looking for the trail moving off to the left through the brush.

Nothing. It wasn't there.

I paced back and forth along the line of chest-high brush growing alongside the path. "It was right here where we turned," I muttered. "It *has* to be…" Finally, I pushed through the undergrowth at the point where the thorns seemed thinnest. The black spikes pulled and scratched at my arms, snagging on my clothes as if trying to stop me. The path we'd followed had gone through the thorn bushes in twenty or thirty feet and then had wound through an open space under the trees for a time. I figured that once through the brush I could pick up the path again even if I was a little to one side or the other of it. The patch of thorns did eventually end, and when I pushed through the last clinging branch, covered with scratches and burrs, I stopped, my eyes narrowing quizzically.

This wasn't where Sheila and I had walked. In fact, it was a part of the woods I recognized quite well. Through the trees, I could glimpse Cooper Creek, a few hundred yards away. I stopped, breathing hard and rubbing at a particularly long and deep scratch on my forearm. "What the fuck is going on here?" I said.

The profanity actually felt good.

I spent the next few hours crisscrossing the area from Cooper Creek to the path. I found nothing, and I was certain that I couldn't possibly have missed anything as large as that ring of chestnut trees had been. Scratched and sweating, I went back to the familiar paths until I found myself behind Mark's house. Through the trees, I could see his window. I sat there, leaning against the gnarled trunk of an old oak, watching, wanting Mark to appear at the window and see me.

He never looked out.

CHAPTER SEVEN

I didn't see Mark or Sheila for two days. I thought I might see Mark at Mass on Sunday, especially since both of our families usually went to the 8:00 Mass. The 10:00 Mass was generally more interesting because old Father Brautski always gave that one to some young visiting priest, who was often far more animated and lively. But going to the earlier Mass meant that we still had the whole day ahead of us, even if we had to pay for that by enduring Father Brautski's boring drone of a sermon. The phone rang around 7:30 and I thought it might be Mark, but it was Dad calling from Pittsburgh; he hadn't been able to come home on Saturday because of some meeting at work.

Mom drove us over to the church. I glanced around as I followed her up the aisle to one of the middle pews, but I didn't see any of the Dyson family there at all. I nodded to school friends and slid into the pew next to Mom. I kept looking back at the entrance as people strolled in until Father Brautski and his two altar boys came out from the vestibule and marched up to the altar in a swirl of organ music, a paean of slightly out-of-tune voices from the choir, and a loud rustling of clothes and a clatter of shifting pews as we all stood.

I glanced behind. No Mark. No Dysons. I turned back to the Mass.

Ambivalence and uncertainty always plagued me in church: in the last year, I'd begun to question the very foundations of my faith. I was no longer certain that I even believed in God at all, though this was a thought I kept well-submerged and never dared to say aloud, even to myself. At the same time, despite my disbelief, I'd look for "signs" in things around me, as if God were taking a personal interest in me and my struggle with belief. I'd loved the medieval overtones and long traditions of the old Latin Mass (especially since I'd been an altar boy myself once and could still recite the *Confiteor* in Latin), but the long High Masses with their incense-scented pomp also tended to put me to sleep. The new Vernacular Mass that the Second Vatican Council and Pope John XXIII had instituted brought in a welcome breath of familiarity, openness and innovation, yet the ceremonies also seemed somehow empty and shallow because of their very modernity.

I went through the habitual routines without paying much attention: standing, sitting, kneeling, mumbling the responses without really hearing them. I was thinking about Mark; I was thinking about Sheila, trying to puzzle out what I was feeling and what was going on.

It was somewhere after the sermon—I don't even know what the topic was as I wasn't paying attention—that I found my gaze snared by one of the statues set in an alcove to the left of the altar: a life-sized image of the Blessed Virgin of the Sacred Heart, dressed Roman-style in a hooded white *stola* with a sky-blue *palla* draped over one shoulder, her hands set delicately between her breasts to display the red, flaming heart painted over the white cloth. Mary, dark-haired but European-fair, was gazing down at the heart and her hands, a beatific expression on her face.

But now she looked up, blinking, as if waking from a deep reverie. I realized that her features were Sheila's, and that she was crying, twin tracks of tears sliding down the glossy cheeks. Her eyes found mine, intent and serious, and her mouth moved. I could lip-read the words she said. "*I'm sorry…*"

I gaped.

"The Virgin—look! She's crying!" The shout came from someone up a few pews in front of us, impossibly loud and startling in the quiet of the church. The mother of one of my classmates was standing, pointing at the statue with a trembling forefinger. Father Brautski lifted his head from his sermon notes, furious at the interruption, but then his gaze followed the shivering gesture to the statue and he audibly gasped. Father Brautski shuffled down from the steps of the altar, past the altar boys who didn't dare move from their kneeling positions. The statue was simply a statue now: unmoving, frozen in the same position as before and looking not at all like Sheila. But…

Father Brautski stood in front of the statue, which now seemed to gaze down at him from its pedestal. The priest stretched out a hand that shook as if with a palsy, lifting it and stretching to touch the painted cheeks with a trembling forefinger. He brought his hand back and gazed at the tip of his finger for several long breaths. Sunlight, coming in through the stained glass windows, caught the drop of moisture there, glittering.

Father Brautski suddenly collapsed to his knees, prostrating himself in front of the statue with his hands clasped in prayer. The church erupted into a hubbub of exclamations and cries as everyone surged out of their pews to move toward the statue.

Shit, I thought, blasphemously.

We didn't get home until afternoon. Mom immediately went to the phone to call Dad and tell him about the miracle in the church. By that time, you'd have thought that the statue had walked out of its alcove and performed a jig in the aisles. People were already claiming to have seen the Virgin move or to speak something specifically for them: Mrs. Taylor, who had suffered for years from arthritis in her hips, claimed to have been healed by the vision, tossing aside the cane she'd carried ever since I'd known her. The church was packed with people trying to view the statue or pray before it, and Father Brautski and the other priests had quickly set up a viewing line and offering box. When we left, Al Schottlekotte, the anchor for Channel Nine news, had already arrived and was interviewing Father Brautski. The diocese's Archbishop was reportedly on his way to act as the public face of the church. A few skeptics in the congregation were talking about humidity and moisture and pinholes in the paint covering the wood.

They were already calling the statue the Weeping Virgin.

I knew better. I knew what I'd seen. There'd been no "miracle"; this was Sheila's doing.

I wanted to talk to Mark, but when I went over to their house the car wasn't in the driveway and no one answered my knock. Maybe they'd gone over to the church to see the statue, or maybe they were just out for a Sunday drive. I headed back for my house. "Hey," a voice said to my left as I started to turn the doorknob.

I glanced over. Sheila was standing at the corner of the house, leaning against the bricks. "Hey," I said back to her.

"I really am sorry," she said with the same expression that had been on the statue's face.

"Sheila, did you...?" I knew the answer.

Her smile was fleeting but wonderful. "I wanted to get your attention." The smile faded again, far too quickly. "Did it work?"

I accepted the admission, though I still wasn't sure. "Do you know the uproar all this caused?" She nodded contritely, but though her mouth was still set in sad frown, I could see a certain satisfaction touch her eyes. "How did you do that? And my God, Sheila, that's a *church*..."

"How?" she answered. "The statue was wood, even if it's dead wood. I can do a lot with wood. Now if it had just been a plaster cast..." She shrugged. "As to it being a church...well, that doesn't mean anything to me. I don't believe in the big old bearded man in the sky, Rob. Besides, who did I hurt? Was your priest upset, or was he excited? Did he look like he wished it had never happened? Did he curse the Virgin Mary for having made the statue cry?"

I scowled, but when I thought about it, she was right. Father Brautski had obviously been ecstatic that the Virgin had chosen to make an appearance at his church, and certainly Mrs. Taylor was pleased with her "cure." Church attendance would be way up for months, and there had been plenty of money stuffed in the offering box next to the statue. Not that I was going to admit that she was right..."You still didn't answer my question," I told her. "*How* did you do it?"

"It was something *you* don't believe in."

"I *saw* it. How can I not believe?"

She laughed at that, a laugh that sounded as it were infused with far more years than she carried, and was utterly devoid of amusement. "If you feel you have to believe everything you see, then you're going to be really confused. People see all sorts of things that aren't real. Dead dogs and wolves, for instance. Or chestnut trees." Her lips turned down. I could see her shoulders sag as if she were tired. She pushed herself away from the bricks. "Look, maybe I should go…"

"No," I told her quickly. "Please. Stay. I haven't seen you in days…"

"So you didn't believe in me anymore?"

I gave an exasperated huff of air. "C'mon. Stop that. You know what I mean. Where have you been?"

A shrug. "I was…out of town. With Mom. We're back now. I should have told you. Another thing I'm sorry about." She gave me another half-smile. "Were you going in or staying out?"

I realized that I was still holding the doorknob. I let go and came down the concrete porch stairs, going over to her. I felt awkward, not quite knowing how I should behave with her now. I wasn't sure of the rules of the game or who was in control of it. If I was uncertain, Sheila wasn't. She immediately hugged me, pulling me to her and putting her head on my shoulder. I held her, marveling, enjoying the feel of her body against mine, the way we pulled each other close.

Her head on my shoulder, she spoke softly into my ear. "If you believe in something, it can happen. Can you believe?" she asked me.

"Yes," I told her. "I think so, anyway."

"Rob, you're hopeless," she said.

Without seeing her face, I wasn't sure of what her inflection meant. I pulled away slightly, so that she glanced up at me. Her ice blue pupils were full of questions. I tilted my head down to hers, and we kissed again. Her mouth was sweet and warm, and I could have stayed like that forever. Her mouth opened under mine. I pulled her tight…

Finally, with a sigh, we broke apart. She smiled at me. "Hi," she said. "That was nice. I take it that my apology's accepted?"

"Yeah. It is."

With that kiss, in that moment, I realized that I was in love, at least as "in love" as someone my age could be. I was filled with it, a white heat that blazed from head to loins, an intensity that I'd never felt before. If you'd asked me then, I would have told you that nothing, nothing at all, could ever change that emotion. Not time, not another person, not distance. Nothing. My love was adamantine, permanent, incorruptible.

Magical.

It felt like anyone's first love felt. I didn't care that I didn't understand her or anything about her. I only cared that she was mine.

"Come on," I said. "We can go into the woods. I want you to show me that place again…"

I took her hand and we started out of my yard, along the low bushes between our house and Mr. Bell's. There was a low growl and a frantic barking as we came near the bushes, and I saw Mr. Bell stick his head out of the front door. He saw us and glared suspiciously in our direction. "Come here, Kitty-Kitty," he said, clapping his hands. The growling receded and a moment later he crouched down on the porch as a gold-brown, low form flecked with gray clambered slowly up the concrete steps and into Mr. Bell's arm. He cradled the dog. It was Kitty-Kitty. I could still see the bloodstains dappling her fur and the way her head waggled dangerously loose on her shoulders. If Mr. Bell noticed any of those things, he said nothing. He stroked her head and glared at me, then went back inside, taking Kitty-Kitty with him.

"Did you do that, too?" I asked Sheila. She shook her head, her thick dark hair swaying.

"No," she told me. "*You* did that, Rob. Not me."

CHAPTER EIGHT

Sheila danced in the high grass, her arms out, her face lifted to the sun, and her eyes closed as she whirled. She laughed, and the sound of her unrestrained joy rebounded from the straight, huge trunks of the chestnuts and rose into the sky like weightless, crystalline, and backward rain.

I still couldn't quite believe that this place existed.

From my house, Sheila and I had gone into the woods along the same paths I'd gone over just the day before, looking for the grove. Only this time, with her leading the way, the brambles and thorns parted at a bend to reveal the narrow path I hadn't been able to find; inexplicably, we passed through to that part of the woods that I'd seen only once before. The ring of chestnut trees hadn't vanished—they were there, still real and genuine: squirrels chattered at us from their high branches and birds roosted in the high topmost crowns. A large crow fluttered down and sat on the lowest branch of the nearest tree, still a good ten feet up from the top of my head. Its ebon head cocked as it stared down at me, fluttering its wings. There was a splash of white at the bird's throat, startling against the midnight of its feathers. It cawed once, opening its yellow beak wide. The hoarse call of the crow was the loudest thing in this world: there seemed to be nothing beyond the ring of trees except primeval forest: no suburbs, no cars, no television sets, no planes in the sky. In the gloom that the trees held in their limbs, I could imagine forms slinking: gray-furred wolves, brown bears, great felines.

I nodded to the crow and went to the tree, placing my hand against the ridges of impossible bark. Solid. Real. Undeniably there. The raven stared, clucking a few times deep in its throat. Its tail lifted and a chalky droplet fell down to land on the toe of my sneaker. "Shit!" I said, glaring up at the bird as I rubbed the sneaker in the grass, still leaning against the tree. The bird cawed again, a derisive laugh.

"Rob, you'd have been a lousy priest."

Sheila's voice, directly behind, startled me and my hand flew away from the tree as if she'd caught me fondling myself. I turned, feeling my face reddening. I glanced again at the bird. "Where'd that come from? Who said I was going to be a priest?"

"You considered it," she answered, the same way someone would say "the sky is blue."

In truth I had—back in eighth grade. I'd gone so far as to have Dad take me over to the parish house to talk to Father Brautski. He'd recited—as dully and emotionlessly as his Sunday sermons— the great wonders of the priestly vocation, and asked me about my 'calling': did I want to be a parish priest, or to go off to convert the heathens, or was I more interested in the monastic life? I stumbled over answers to which I really hadn't given much thought. I told him I wanted to be a priest like him, which in most unpriestly fashion was a flat-out lie. I most assuredly did *not* want to be like Father Brautski, but neither of his other two options sounded particularly pleasant. Stereotypical images fluttered through my head: I couldn't see myself in Africa or India or China, tending to my malnourished flock in a fly-infested village, nor could I imagine myself happy in my tonsure and itchy woolen robe, hands pressed together as I knelt in a tiny stone cell and prayed in silence. Being a parish priest seemed the most appealing of the options he'd given me.

Still, my statement made Father Brautski's face wrinkle in the nearest approximation of a smile I'd ever seen in his face, and he nodded to my father. I was moderately surprised that a bolt of lightning didn't arc crackling through the windows and strike me dead right there. In the end, Father Brautski patted me on the shoulders, shook my Dad's hand, and told Dad that if I were still interested at the end of the year, he would give him the name of someone to contact for seminary high school. And about two weeks later, walking home with one of the neighborhood girls and feeling the pull of hormonal surges, I realized that while my intellect might have been curious about the priesthood, my body was most assuredly curious about other, more worldly things.

At the end of the year, I never did go back to talk to Father Brautski.

"And why would I be a lousy priest?" I asked Sheila.

She didn't answer except by sliding a forefinger slowly down my chest. Somewhere between the end of my ribcage and navel, I stopped breathing. The finger halted just above the belt of my jeans, pressing into me there. "Because you don't have Faith," Sheila said as I blinked at her and let out the breath I was holding. I could hear the capital-F she put on the last word. "You question everything you see and you want to know how it works and why. Oh, you might have managed to be a half-decent Jesuit if you'd had to: they're the closest you can come to pragmatic, logical realists. But even that…" She pulled her hand away, taking a step back from me. I could still feel the sensation of her fingertip on my abdomen. "You're not happy with the way things are, but you can't just accept that what you want is all around you. You can't just believe; you have to ask questions."

"Since when is establishing whether something's actually true or not wrong?"

The crow chortled above us, shuffling down the branch with a fluttering of wings. I could no longer see the flash of white at its throat; I wondered whether another bird had exchanged places with it while we'd been talking. "Shut up, Elisa," Sheila said to it, glancing up. The crow cawed back at her, leaning over the branch.

"Elisa?" I asked her. That brought Sheila's gaze back down to me. Cobalt under night-black, she regarded me.

"There's something wrong with that name?" she said, with enough of a lift at the end of the sentence to add an unspoken… *and what about it…?*

"My Mom'd be really pissed if I named a crow after her."

"Then it's a good thing you haven't," Sheila answered. She extended her arm, palm facing the ground. The crow stirred, gliding down from the branch to land on her wrist like a falcon to its handler. Sheila crooned to it, reaching over with her other hand to stroke its bright, dark head. The bird let her touch it, undisturbed, and then flew off as she lifted her arm again. It circled the grove of chestnuts, rising higher until it vanished in the high branches.

"How long did it take you to tame the crow?" I asked. "That's cool—" I stopped, seeing her frown.

"It's not tame," she said. "Believe me. She does what she wants."

"But the way you called it down..." I shook my head.

Sheila pressed her lips together. "What is it you want, Rob? I mean, what in your life do you really, really *want*?"

I'm looking at it, I could have told her. I didn't know what I was feeling when I was with her, but I knew it was different than anything I'd experienced before, and I knew I'd been feeling it almost from the moment I first saw her. I didn't know whether to call it infatuation, lust, or love—it was something I'd never experienced before. She wasn't my ideal of beauty, wasn't the type of girl I usually fantasized about at night. But what I did know was that when I was with Sheila, the sunlight appeared brighter and the colors around me seemed more saturated and real. There was an emptiness and grayness inside me when she wasn't there. Even as I thought them, the words seemed overblown and sophomorically dramatic—pure clichés of romance—but that didn't alter the truth that this was the way I felt.

But I didn't say any of that. Maybe that was my mistake. Even then, in that singular moment, I was questioning myself. I told myself that yeah, it might be different, but the feelings would change and wither and die, just as they had with every other girl I'd been with so far. Despite my conviction only a few hours ago when we'd kissed, now I was certain that this phase wouldn't last. Couldn't last. It was just a fascination, the newness...

I was entirely wrong in that. But that was something I wouldn't realize for a long time yet.

Sheila was staring at me, and I answered obliquely. "I don't want to go to Pittsburgh," I said. "I want to stay here."

"Why?" she asked.

"Don't you know?"

The barest wisp of a smile touched her lips and danced through her eyes. "I can make a guess. But I'd rather you told me."

I never realized honesty was so hard. I had to try twice to get the words out, and when I did, they were halting and slow. "It's... it's *you*, Sheila. I don't want to leave here because this is where you are."

For the first time, she seemed almost shy, her gaze dropping away from me for a moment. The crow cawed from the trees and Sheila glanced up at it, her chest rising in a sigh she released audibly. "Then maybe you shouldn't leave."

I gave an exasperated huff of air. "I have to."

"You can always affect your own life, just like I can affect mine. After all, your parents don't really want to go to Pittsburgh, any more than you do. You all want the same thing, and that makes it much easier." Her face went somber. "A lot easier than Mark has it."

I grimaced at the reminder of Mark. "I don't have a choice," I insisted.

"We always have choices," she told me. "And often enough, that's the problem."

Sheila left me before we left the woods, where the path forked away toward South Crest, near the log I'd once seen her using as a drum. "Where you going?"

"Home," she said. "For a bit. I'll see you tomorrow. Think about what you want."

"I am," I told her, and pulled her to me. We kissed, and when I tried to hold on to her she laughed and pushed me away.

"Go on now," she said. I grinned at her and walked on. She stood there on the path watching me walk toward the noise of the afternoon lawnmowers. I glanced behind once; she waved at me. As I started to turn a corner where a tangle of blackberry bushes would finally hide her from view, she was gone.

I came out of the woods and started walking back up the street to my house, but as I reached Mr. Bell's house, I stopped and stared at our lawn. Something was different, and for a minute I couldn't place it. Then it struck me: the FOR SALE sign Mom had put up was missing. I half-ran to the door and looked in at the front room. "Hey, Mom…" I began. Stopped.

The bookcase…Dad had built the bookcase when they'd first moved here. I'd been only about four at the time, but I still remembered him putting together the frame, drilling holes in the wall and hammering plastic anchors into the holes, then screwing the whole massive structure into place. It had covered the entire wall of the front room, eight feet high and a good twelve feet long. My back still ached remembering the two days it had taken to box the books and move them down to the basement.

"Why?" I'd asked when Mom said we had to take the bookcase down. "That'd be a selling point for me. You too—you read all the time."

Mom was already shaking her head. "We read, but most people don't have as many books as we do, and they don't want their living room looking like a library. No, the house will sell better if they just see a wall there and can decorate it however they want…" So Dad and I had boxed the books and disassembled the bookcase.

But the bookcase *wasn't* gone. It was there. I stood in front of it, gaping at the shelves of colorful spines and smelling their faint must. I could see the *Golden Guide To Trees*, in which I'd looked up the leaves of the chestnut tree, and the faux-leather spines of the encyclopedia. Not in boxes any longer, but back where they'd once been.

"What?" Mom asked me, coming in from the kitchen. She saw me looking at the bookcase and glanced at the shelves herself. "Something the matter, Rob? Oh, yes, you're right; that really needs a good dusting…"

I started to say something, to stutter my amazement, but in staring at the bookcase, I noticed that Mom was right: the shelves were dusty with visible cobwebs in the back corners. I remembered them: I'd wiped them away as we'd shelved the books.

The bookcase hadn't been there this morning when I'd gone through the room, and even if Mom had somehow been so industrious as to put it back up while I'd been walking in the woods with Sheila, there hadn't been time for the dust or the house spiders. I shook my head, expecting to find myself waking from some extraordinarily vivid dream, but everything stayed there.

She was wiping her hands on her apron. "You should go wash up. Supper's almost ready, and your father will be home in a few minutes."

"Dad? I thought he was in Pittsburgh."

She cocked her head at me as if I'd just grown a second nose. "Pittsburgh? Whatever would make you think that?" She was staring, and I forced a laugh.

"Just kidding," I told her. She continued to stare. "You know. A joke."

"Uh-huh." She was still wiping her hands, though her eyebrows had knotted.

"All right," I told her. "I guess I'll go clean up now." I walked past her into the bathroom, glancing into the kitchen. Mom and Dad painted those walls back in May, changing the bright yellow to a more neutral off-white, so that the new owners could paint the kitchen whatever color they might want. Like the bookcase, the yellow walls had also returned. I felt disoriented and a bit nauseous. I hurried past Mom hoping she wouldn't notice.

I went into the bathroom and locked the door behind me. I sat on the toilet cover for a long time.

When I came out, the bookcase was still there, the kitchen walls were still yellow, and Dad was striding through the front door, whistling.

CHAPTER NINE

When I finally did see Mark, he didn't want to talk to me.

I saw him in his front yard as I came out of the house the next morning, sitting on the steps of his front porch. I walked across the street toward him (glancing once at our own yard, where the sign was somehow still missing, and where Dad was walking out of the house to go to work). Mark looked up as I reached the curb and I thought that I saw a purplish bruise across one cheek, though at that distance, I suppose it might have been a shadow. Mark seemed to grimace and he pulled himself to his feet, one hand on the wrought iron railing, walking up the steps toward the front door. "Mark!" I called. "C'mon, man…We need to talk."

He didn't say anything, didn't even look back at me. He went into the house as I stopped on the grass between curb and sidewalk. The door shut behind him with finality. I stood there for a few minutes, staring at their house as if Mark might come back out or I might see him at one of the windows.

Then I finally turned and headed back to my house. I dragged myself morosely to the porch steps. Through the plate glass window of the house, I could see Mom dusting the bookcase and hear the faint thump of the music she was playing as she worked. I wanted to see Sheila again, and decided I should head over to South Crest, but a voice intruded even as I turned.

"Hey."

Sheila was there, leaning against the corner of our house.

"Hey," I said back to her.

"I like the way your yard looks now," she said. "It's not so…cluttered." She smiled at me, but the expression faded in almost the same moment and her lips pressed together.

"How did you…?" I gestured to where the sign had been.

"Wasn't me." She shrugged, still reclining against the house. "You were the one who wanted it, remember? It's easy to make someone do what they want to do. People do that all the time, without even knowing it."

"Not like this." I glanced into the house again, at the bookcase. Mom was gone, though the music was still playing. "All last night, I kept waiting for everything to change back, to snap back to the way it was, like a rubber band that had been stretched too far."

She shrugged. "It still could. Depends on what you really want." I saw her glance across the street, narrowing her eyes.

"Have you managed to talk to Mark?" I asked. She shook her head. She pushed away from the house and moved toward me with a single step. She seemed morose and solemn today, so unlike her usual self. I wondered whether something had happened to her, whether she and her mom had an argument. With even more paranoia, I wondered whether she'd changed her mind about me.

The thought of that possibility hurt, physically. I took her hands in mine, and couldn't help glancing once at the picture window of the front room just to see if Mom had come back into the room and might be there watching. Sheila saw my glance; she shook her head, just a bare shake accompanied by a tightening of her lips. She started to pull her hands away from mine. I held on, desperately, and she sighed, finally seeming to surrender. I wanted to talk about us, but that was too dangerous a topic.

"I just saw Mark," I told Sheila. "He walked right back into the house when he saw me coming and wouldn't talk to me. But I thought…" I took in a long breath, wondering whether I wanted to tell her the rest. "I thought I saw a bruise on his face."

I'd expected her to be upset by that, but her response surprised me. Her eyes filled with quick tears. "Hey," I said, releasing one hand to brush at them with my thumb. "He's okay now. He didn't look too hurt."

The tears spilled over, and Sheila sniffed, shaking her head. "He's going to get hurt worse if you don't help him, Rob. You have to do something."

"What?" I asked. "What can I do? I wanted to report it, honest I did, but I was afraid that if the cops didn't do something, then JD would *really* beat the crap out of Mark in retaliation. Wouldn't matter to him who told—he'd take it all out on Mark. I don't know what to do." I pressed her hands in mine. "Unless maybe *you...*" I began, thinking of the bookcase and my parents, of Kitty-Kitty and the statue at the church, but my voice trailed off as I saw the bloom of irritation in her face.

"You still don't understand, do you?" she told me. "You don't understand who's in control of it all." She pulled her hands away from me, half-turning. "I can't believe this. I can't believe how wrong this is all turning out."

"It's not your fault."

Her face told me that she didn't believe that at all. "Rob, you don't know. You just don't know." She looked over at Mark's house again. "We need to talk to him. We need to find out what he wants us to do."

"He won't talk to me," I repeated. "Not right now. That's pretty clear."

"Then you need to try again. You have to, Rob." Her face was serious, her eyes searching mine. "It's so very important."

I took a breath, pulling myself away from her to look at Mark's house. "All right," I told her. "I'll try again. Meet me in the woods afterward? At the gateway?"

She nodded and kissed me quickly—a brush of lips that, disappointingly, held no erotic promise at all. I headed over to Mark's house, my feet feeling heavier with each step and my guts twisting tighter.

"Tell Mark I really need to talk with him."

Jackie had already called upstairs once to Mark. I'd heard Mark's growl in response: "Tell him to go f..." A pause. Then: "...just go away."

I wasn't moving even though Jackie had half-closed the door. "It's important," I said. "I really gotta talk to him." She gave me a look of disgust and stomped back into the house. I heard her yell up to Mark, heard him say something in return that I couldn't hear this time. Jackie came back to the door.

"He said to tell the asshole to come on up then," she said.

"A ten-year-old little girl shouldn't talk like that," I told her.

"I'm eleven," she told me. "And *I* didn't say it. Mark did."

I went into the house. I thought I could hear a television going in the downstairs bedroom—probably Mrs. Dyson. JD wasn't home, I hoped. I hadn't been in the house for a while. It smelled of yesterday's dinner, and my parents would have thrown a fit at the state of the living room: Jackie's toys all over the floor, old clothes tossed over the backs of chairs, half-empty glasses and paper plates on the coffee table. I went up the stairs to the second floor: two bedrooms, one Jackie's, the other Mark's. His door was shut; *Vanilla Fudge* was playing loud on his stereo. I knocked. "Yeah?" I heard Mark's voice from the other side.

"It's me. Rob."

"Come in if that's what you really want."

I opened the door. He was laying on his bed, rolled on his side facing away from me. There was a smell in the room, a spice in the air that I didn't recognize then and a hint of fading blue smoke. His window was open, a fan set on the sill blowing out. He didn't speak until I closed the door.

"So…are the two of you screwing?"

The obscenity reddened my face as if he'd slapped it. "Jesus, Mark…"

"I'll bet she'd like that, slamming your cock into her wet little cunt while she wraps her legs around you. Does she suck your dick, too?"

"Shut *up*, man." A year or so ago, Mark had given me a tattered paperback book with the cover half torn off. "*Found it in the basement in one of Dad's old toolboxes. Read it—just don't let your parents see it…*" Now Mark was talking like the narrator of that book, spouting the filth and the words and the acts we knew from books but not from life. I couldn't have said those phrases, not like

85

that—casually, as if I were talking about the weather. "Just…shut up," I said again. I didn't know what else to say.

He didn't turn, didn't respond, just kept talking. "And hell, you don't even have to worry about her mom finding out or even breaking up with her, 'cause you're gone after this summer anyway. So you can just screw your brains out and then say 'Hey, that was nice. Well, gotta go. See ya.' Or was your moving just another lie like the rest? I notice the sign's gone. Maybe you two can bang all the way to Christmas."

"Shut the fuck *up*, Mark!" I yelled it, so loudly that I was surprised his mother or Jackie didn't come to see what was the matter. I suppose they were used to yelling and obscenities in that house, though. Mark rolled on the bed to look at me.

The bruise still mottled his cheek. His eyes were baggy and dark and slitted, and they stared at me with the dead, flat gaze of a snake. The whites of his eyes were shot through with red, broken veins. "What's the matter, buddy? The truth hurt?"

"None of it's true, Mark, and you know it."

"I saw you in the woods, man. I know what the fuck you were doing. Don't goddamn lie to me."

"We kissed each other. That's what you saw. And yeah, she likes me and I like her. I'm not going to apologize for that. We'd have told you about it, too, if you'd given us a chance. She's *your* friend, too, you know."

"Yeah. She's got a great way of showing me just how good a friend she is."

"I'm not gonna let you talk about her like that. I'm not."

"Or what? You gonna beat me up, Rob? You gonna give me a whippin'? You gonna protect your precious woman from all those bad things I'm saying about her? You gonna stop me from calling her a slut or a whore? You think I'm at all scared of you?"

He'd sat up in the bed, swinging his legs over the side, his face all twisted up, his mouth just a tight line and angry creases at the corner of his eyes and across his nose, his hands balled into fists at his side. I thought he was going to bound off the bed toward me, and I took a step back, bringing my hands in front in mute defense. He glared. Then all the fury left him; he lay back on the bed again, his eyes closed. "Nobody's ever gonna touch me again like that," he said. A single tear leaked from under his closed eyelids. "No-fucking-body."

"I don't want that, either," I told him. My fisted hands relaxed. "Mark, man...I want to help you. Tell me what I can do."

"You can't help. This is all my fucking problem."

"We could go to the police, me and Sheila. I'd do that. Heck, I could get my parents to come with us—my folks have been about to do that a couple times anyway. They can stop it. We can stop it."

Mark's eyes opened. "How? By putting my dad in jail? That'd be a big goddamn help. He's always talking about how far behind we are on the fucking bills, how we're drowning in debt. Put Dad in jail and he'll lose the fucking lousy job he already has. Hell, half the time already he doesn't go to work 'cause he hates it so much; he just calls in sick and sits watching the TV. Or maybe they'd take me and Jackie away from him and put us in a foster home. That'd be great, too—stick us somewhere with people we don't know, probably two different families even if they can find anyone to take us at all at our ages. Or maybe the cops'll just come and talk to Dad. Now wouldn't that be just peachy, because he'd be nice and polite and normal-looking while they were here, telling them how it all must be some silly mistake, and Mom would just sit there shaking her head and smiling and not saying anything either, while all the time Dad would be just boiling inside and getting more and more fucking pissed, and after they leave, wondering why the fuck they even had to come here to talk with this nice polite guy who obviously loves his family, Dad'd be so goddamn furious he'd *really* go off on me. Yeah, those are great solutions you have, Rob. They're just fucking wonderful."

Mark sat up, more slowly this time. His hands lay on his lap, palms up, squeezing and relaxing as if he were trying to crush the words he was saying. "You don't see him afterward, Rob. You don't hear him tell me how awfully sorry he is that he hit me. You don't see him fucking crying his alligator tears. You don't see him come up here at night and begging me to forgive him. 'I got this bad temper, Mark. That's all. A goddamn bad temper that sometimes I can't control. You understand that, don't you, son? You understand

87

I don't mean nothin' by it? You know how much I care about all of you.' Oh, I understand, all right. I understand that he always got mad, real fast. I understand that he used to whale the tar out of my ass with his hand or a belt when I did something wrong as a little kid. And I understand that in the last two or three years he's started hitting me with his fucking fists. I understand all that real good." He touched his face. "I understand it perfectly."

I blinked. "Then maybe someone can get him some help, teach him to control his temper, get him some medicine or something to keep him calm..."

Mark was shaking his head. "You still don't get it, do you? 'Cause y'know, I don't think he's really sorry at all. I think he's just fucking *scared* after he hurts one of us, scared someone's going to find out about what he's doing. When he's hitting me, I look at his face, and there's a damn *joy* in his eyes, almost a smile on his face, like this is something that he really, really gets a kick out of. He doesn't want to change the way he is. You know what? I think he'd actually like to be that way more often. I think he has a fucking orgasm from it. It was always me he hit before, never Mom or Jackie; the last time, he slapped Mom, too, when she started screaming that he should stop. I'll bet he enjoyed that. I'll bet he fucked her afterward, just 'cause he wanted to. I figure soon enough he'll start on Jackie, too."

My eyebrows had climbed somewhere near my hairline. "Mark, he isn't the devil, man. He's your dad. He's got a problem, yeah, but—"

"No," Mark interrupted loudly. "*I* got the problem, and my problem's him. I'll tell you what I've figured out—there's only one goddamn way to deal with it: when someone hurts you, you just hurt them back harder."

He was literally shaking, his knees drawn up almost to his chest, his face a carved mask of internal fury and frustration. I sat on the edge of the bed near him, reaching out to touch his arm, and he jerked himself away. I brought my hand back. "Mark, we can figure out a way to deal with this. All of us. Together. You gotta let us help."

He lay on his side, facing the wall, still curled up. "It's *my* prob-lem," I heard him say. "I'll figure it out. And if either of you two assholes say anything, I'll fucking beat the crap out of both of you."

"Mark—"

"I mean it, man. You want to be my friend? Then leave it alone. That's what I want you to do. Leave it alone."

And I did. God help me, I did.

CHAPTER TEN

I held my hand over the stones of the gateway, staring down at the smooth, polished surface spattered with flecks of Kitty-Kitty's dried blood. I remembered the surprise of seeing Sheila suddenly standing just beyond them, the heat I'd felt when she placed my hand on them just a few days ago.

Grimacing, I slapped my hand palm down on top of the column, ready to snatch it away again if I felt heat.

The stones were cold. Dead cold.

I'd been there half an hour. Finally, I sat down with my back to one of the columns, closing my eyes—not sleeping, just listening to the woods around me. I could hear everything: the versatile, long song of a mockingbird a few trees over, the frantic scurrying of a pair of squirrels in the branches above me, the hammer taps of a woodpecker down in the valley, the violin-bow scraping of leaves as a breeze swayed the tops of the trees, the trilling of cicadas. I could hear the sounds of the nearby houses as well: the shush of neighborhood traffic, the distant barking of dogs, the yells from a game of baseball in someone's backyard.

"I'm either a lot quieter than you think, or you're the world's soundest sleeper."

Startled at the sound of the voice, I opened my eyes. Sheila was crouching in front of me, her face only inches from mine. "So which is it?" she asked.

"Neither. I think you just appeared because I wanted you so much."

To her credit, she didn't grimace or laugh at my overblown and hackneyed reply, preserving my dignity even as I wished I could have that one back. "I'll take that," she said. Her face was serious and unsmiling, but she leaned forward, kissing my forehead. "How's Mark?" she asked. She sat back with her legs folded underneath her. I took a long, slow breath before answering. I wasn't going to tell her what he'd actually said, and I wondered whether I could lie convincingly to her.

"He's hurting," I said. "In a lot of ways." Her hand lifted and fell back into her lap as if stricken, as if she wanted to interrupt, though she didn't. "He...thinks I betrayed him."

She sniffed, looking away and blinking hard. "He thinks *I* betrayed him," she corrected me. "And he's right to blame me."

"You? Blame you for what? Mark's an idiot if he thinks..."

Sheila put her hand on my leg and that stopped my burgeoning tirade. "You're his friend, Rob. You've been his friend for years. He knows that. Me, I'm the new one. He doesn't know me. He doesn't really even see me as a person—I'm this girl he's interested in. I'm not 'Sheila,' I'm someone he wants but doesn't know. He doesn't know whether he can trust me."

"I trust you." It sounded stupid. It was also all I could think to say.

She shook her head. "Maybe you shouldn't be so certain of that, either."

I knew that mostly I was just scared: scared of Mark, scared of caring so much for both of them because I knew that someone had to be hurt here, that there was no way to avoid the pain for someone or maybe all of us.

"Talk to him again," Sheila said. "Try. Keep trying until he listens."

"Sheila..." I began to say, and in that word was all the fear, all the uncertainty, all the tangled emotions I felt at that moment. Her hands found mine, grasping them.

"You have to try," she said, and pulled me toward her. "Please, Rob. I wish, I wish..." I leaned forward and kissed her again, and this time the heat of her mouth drove away all the specters. I clenched her tightly, rolling us both down onto the ground, still lost in that kiss, wanting to stay there forever, trying to obliterate all the possible futures with one eternal present. Our tongues touched, and I felt the strangely pleasant tightness in my groin that I'd felt before while making out with Debbie earlier in the year. One arm under her, I let the other drift up from her waist, resting it on her stomach, my fingers just under the hem of her blouse. Slowly, slowly as we continued to kiss, I let my hand slide upward underneath her T-shirt, half-expecting her hand to move and to stop me at any second. My fingertips stroked the underside of her breast captured in the lacy fabric of her bra. I stopped; I'd never touched a woman's breast before.

I pulled slightly away from Sheila, looking down at her, lost in the blue of her searching eyes, my fingers till grazing the underside of her breast. There was no warning there, no refusal. We kissed again, and I moved my hand up, cupping her fully. Her hand found mine, pressing me against her. I heard her shuddering intake of breath, felt her nipple rising under the thin tricot of the bra. Her hips lifted, pushing against me. Then she gently pushed my hand away and sat up. "No," she said. "We can't. Not yet. Maybe never."

"Sorry," I whispered.

"Don't be, Rob. It's just…right now…" For the first time, I realized that Sheila wasn't so much different than me, that she was less than confident and self-assured. I realized that she was as scared of what the future held as I was, and I loved her more than before for showing me that vulnerability. And as the sexual heat receded a bit, I realized that I was glad she'd stopped us, too—because I wasn't sure what to do next or how far to take things, or what to do if they went further. We'd reached and pushed past the boundaries of my little experience. Everything beyond here was new and unexplored, frightening and exhilarating at the same time.

I was as scared as she was. Probably more.

"It's okay. I understand." I brushed her face. My fingers still tingled with the feel of her breast. I could imagine the soft, soft flesh, the sloping of skin…I kissed her again.

It was just a kiss. The moment had gone, and we both realized it. We didn't say anything as we left the woods, holding hands.

CHAPTER ELEVEN

"Leave it alone," Mark had said when we'd talked. So I left it alone.

Mark managed to get himself ungrounded a few days later, mostly because he was so bored and contentious that his mother obviously wanted him out of the house.

"Is Rob home?" I heard Mark's voice at our front door, and I half ran, half slid down the stairs from my room as Mom let him in. I could see her looking at him carefully; all but the ghosts of the bruises had faded and his face didn't look much worse than any acne-riddled teenage boy's. He was staring at the bookcase in the living room in the same startled way I had, but said nothing.

"Haven't seen you around the last few days, Mark," Mom ventured, and got the careful shrug I knew was coming.

"Grounded," he said.

Mom waited, but no further elucidation was coming. Finally, she nodded. "Oh, here's Rob," she said, as if noticing me for the first time. "Say hi to your mother for me, would you, Mark? We haven't talked in a while. Tell her... Tell her she should come over for lunch or something. I'd like to chat with her."

"Sure. I'll tell her."

Mom nodded, smiled absently at the two of us, and left the room. Mark looked at the bookcase again and nodded toward the door. "Let's take a walk."

Outside, we headed into the woods, cutting across Mr. Bell's backyard. Kitty-Kitty yapped at us from inside the house. At the sound, Mark stopped for a second as he was about to vault the chain-link fence, his hand on the gray aluminum rail. Mr. Bell came to the back screen door, holding Kitty-Kitty. "Get out of my yard, you two hooligans!" he shouted at us. He set the dog down. Kitty-Kitty growled and bared her teeth behind the torn screen as Mr. Bell opened the door. We hopped the fence as the dachshund barked and half-ran, half-waddled toward us.

Mark stopped on the other side of the fence and crouched there as Kitty-Kitty tried to push herself through the links. "I killed you once before," Mark whispered to the dog. "I can do it again. Go on. Just give me the slightest fucking reason."

Kitty-Kitty stopped yapping and whined once. The dog looked at me, its expression changing, and I was half-afraid it was going to talk to me again and I didn't know if I wanted Mark to hear that. Or maybe I didn't want to know whether Mark also heard the dog's voice. Mark grinned and slapped me on the back.

I followed him quickly into the woods.

There'd been thunderstorms the night before; under the trees, our dirt paths were dark and damp. We both saw the sneaker prints as we hit the fork that led over to South Crest. "Hey, look at the size—that's gotta be Sheila…" Mark said, his voice sounding too casual. "Not long ago, either. Let's see if we can catch up with her."

I didn't think anyone could catch Sheila unless she wanted to be caught, but I followed him anyway, as always blundering along behind him. He was acting for all the world as if nothing had happened in the last few weeks, as if he'd never seen Sheila and me together, as if he'd never been beaten by his dad, as if the world was unchanged from the way it had been before this summer started. For a moment, remembering the bookcase in our front room, I wondered whether that was really the case, but then I saw the way the muscles were clenched in his jaw and the steely set of his eyes, and I knew better.

I wondered how long the illusion could last.

It wasn't hard to catch Sheila. She was waiting for us, leaning against a large, mossy boulder next to the creek. I went past Mark and stood next to her, finding her hand. I could feel her hesitation. She moved her hand away and then back again, and this time her fingers closed around mine. I watched Mark, whose gaze had dropped to our linked hands. Now his eyes lifted and regarded me for several seconds. He scuffed at the leaves on the ground and glanced away to the roof of trees overhead, the sun raining haloed spots of light down on us. He nodded as if acknowledging what he saw.

"Nice day for a hike," he said. "Let's head down to Cooper Creek."

I glanced at Sheila; she shrugged. "Sure," I said. "Why not?"

"All right," Mark said. "Let's go..."

For a while then, it was as if nothing had ever happened between us. Mark and I could have been a few years younger, and Sheila just a friend we knew and had allowed to accompany us. Mark sang and howled, cussed and cavorted as we had all the summers before. He stripped two branches from a dead tree, tossed one to me, and we capered over and around fallen trees performing a mock sword fight that ended with an overly dramatic death by Mark. He leaped to a low-hanging branch, swung by his hands and dropped down again, taking me to the ground with him, laughing. He picked up a red-capped mushroom from the loamy soil under a decaying log, pretended to eat it, and died again to our applause. He stopped us with a dramatic finger to his mouth. "Listen..." he said with a serious expression on his face, and when we quieted and were listening with held breaths, he roared suddenly, guffawing at our expressions and running from me when I chased him, laughing.

If I noticed that most of the time he acted as if Sheila weren't there and directed all his attention to me, I didn't remark on it. I was just glad to have the old Mark back. I wasn't about to question why he'd returned—whether it was another one of the strange occurrences of this summer or just an act.

We reached Cooper Creek and started following it upstream, skipping rocks across the patches of deeper water, hopping from rock to rock over the narrower stretches where the water moved quickly over the rocks. We chased minnows through the shallows, tried to sneak up—unsuccessfully—on the bulbous-eyed bullfrogs sitting on the muddy banks, caught slow-moving tadpoles in our hands and looked at the legs just starting to sprout at the base of their tails.

A half mile or so up the creek, we reached the place Mark and I had christened Big Bend.

Big Bend was where Cooper Creek, running south at that point, turned abruptly ninety degrees to the west. There, the flowing water had carved out a thirty-foot-high bluff into the hill on the outside of the bend's elbow. This was the deepest part of the creek, waist- to chest-high in the channel that ran under the wall of dirt, clay and stone. The trees at the top of the bluff were old and venerable, their root systems looping in and out of the dirt of the cliff, their branches overhanging the water, and from those branches thick vines hung. We'd swung on them a thousand times over the years, swinging out high over the creek with yells and shrieks, the branches dropping us a startling few feet as we took running starts and kicked off from the edge of the bluff. "Hey, come on!" Mark called to me as he ran up the slope of the bluff. Sheila stayed below at the creek, turning over rocks as if she were looking for salamanders or snakes.

I followed Mark. By the time I reached the top of the bluff, he already had a vine in his hands and was taking a running start, leaping off the edge of the cliff and swinging out over the curve of Big Bend with a whoop and a holler that rang over the shallow water and the rock-strewn banks. The branch above him creaked and groaned, dipping and swaying with Mark's weight, and he came onto the bluff in a crash of leaves and twigs. He handed me the vine. "Your turn, Tarzan," he said. He grinned, like the old Mark.

I tugged on the vine to make sure it would take my weight— both Mark and I had failed to test vines before and had the vine pull off the tree entirely. The ropy wood seemed solid enough. I grabbed the vine in both hands and ran toward the cliff edge. As I pushed off, I dropped a foot or two, my weight pulling the vine and branch down. The feeling in the pit of my stomach was exhilarating, a rush like the first drop of a roller coaster, and I yelled at the sheer joy of it. The world swung by in a whirl of green and blue and brown, my feet kicking as I arced high over the creek, then lifting my legs so I'd swing back over the lip of bluff.

Just before I reached the ground once more, I suddenly dropped again, a good two feet. My feet touched the edge of the cliff, but my body went backward out over the creek as I held desperately onto the vine. "Shit!" I shouted, and I heard Sheila scream in alarm from below. I swayed, almost laying flat in the air, my body out over nothing but air and the heels of my sneakers just holding onto the grassy summit. I heard the vine creaking above me and my body dropped another few inches, my head now lower than my feet. Then I saw Mark—or his left hand, anyway—reach out and grasp the vine three feet above my hands as he held onto one of the small trees for support. Above me, I could see that most of the tendrils of the vine had snapped away from the branch, and I knew that if Mark let go, the vine would probably not hold my weight. I'd fall, probably head-first, twenty feet to water far too shallow, to the rocks piled at the base of the cliff. If I were lucky, I'd break a leg or arm. If I were unlucky, I'd be dead or paralyzed. "Mark!" I yelled. "Don't let go, man! Pull me up!"

Lifting my head, I could see him. He was grinning, his face looking adult and fierce, his eyes narrowed. "You know what, Rob?" he said, far too calmly. "If I let go, you get to do a high dive into the creek. Ouch, that'd be bad, wouldn't it?"

"Mark, damn it! Pull me up!"

He didn't answer, just continued to talk in a soft monotone. I could hear Sheila thrashing her way up toward us, shouting. "This is what it feels like, Rob, when someone else has control over you—just like I'm holding you up right now. This is what it feels like every time I see my dad with that craziness in his eyes. You hang there, and you know that you'll live or die depending on what that person does. It sucks, doesn't it? You know what, if I let go right now, no one would blame me. No, I'd be the fucking tragic hero of the tale, the brave teen who tried to rescue his good friend and just couldn't quite hang on. And Sheila…I'll bet she'd need someone to comfort her, wouldn't she? I'll bet, that after a little bit, we'd be more. It'd be a natural progression, don't you think? The guy who tried to save his friend gets the girlfriend. Kind of like an inheritance from you."

I could see his arm, the corded muscles quivering with tension and weariness, and I knew he couldn't hold onto the vine much longer. He lifted me up a foot or so, but kept me swaying out over the cliff so that my scrabbling, sneaker-clad feet couldn't get purchase on the ground; if he dropped me now, I'd freefall those inches and tear the vine entirely loose from its fragile moorings. "Mark, please!"

"I don't know, Rob," he answered. "Why is it that you get what you want when I was the one who brought her here? Huh? Answer me that."

"Mark, you're talking crazy."

He grinned. "You think she could she bring you back, Rob? Like Kitty-Kitty? You could be her zombie lover. What do you think? Maybe we should find out. That'd be interesting." He jiggled the vine; leaves fluttered down and the vine ripped away from the branch entirely. All that held me up now was Mark's hand.

"Mark!"

I caught a glimpse of Sheila, running up toward us. Mark must have heard her, too. With a grunt of effort, he pulled hard on the vine, finally pulling me up and in. I slid onto solid ground. I collapsed then, smelling the moldy, wonderful odor of loamy earth, my breath loud and fast.

"Man, that was fucking close," Mark declared loudly, shaking his head down at me as if he'd said nothing at all to me a few seconds ago. He reached down with his hand as Sheila came up behind him. "You're all right now, buddy," he said. "Everything's fine now."

Sheila was standing alongside him, her hand on his arm, looking down at me with concern. "Rob?"

"I'm OK," I said. I ignored Mark's hand and stood up, brushing leaves and dirt from my clothes. "Let's get the hell out of here." I started walking away, not even looking at Mark, not wanting to see what was on his face.

"Rob!" Sheila called behind me. "How can you just walk away like that? Mark just saved you from a terrible fall."

I turned. She was standing alongside him. Mark was grinning. He spread his hands like a performer asking for the audience's heartfelt applause.

"Yeah, thanks a fucking ton," I managed to grunt, then turned away again, kicking at the leaves as I headed down the hill.

CHAPTER TWELVE

We said nothing on the way out. I strode out of the woods angry and well ahead of the two of them. I could hear Mark and Sheila conversing behind me. Mark's mom called for him almost as soon as he reached the street again, and Mark scowled and yelled back to her. "*Coming!* I'll be right back," he said to Sheila. "Don't go anywhere." He smiled at her, gave me a hard-eyed grin. Sheila hugged him. I sat on my porch steps, glowering at his retreating back, the concrete hard and warm under me.

"What's the matter with you?" Sheila asked. "Why are you so angry?"

"Mark," I managed to spit out. "He was going to let me drop. He wanted to hurt me."

"What do you mean?" I could hear the disbelief in Sheila's voice. "Rob, I was there watching. If Mark hadn't pulled you in, you'd have fallen. I saw it. I saw it all."

She sat next to me, the shadow of the pin oak in the yard cool over us. I leaned my head back on the wrought-iron railing, looking up at the pattern of leaves against the sky.

"You didn't hear what he was saying to me, Sheila," I said. "He was whispering all this crazy shit. Crazy."

"Rob, he saved you from a nasty fall. You can't deny that."

"Yeah, he did. But he also made sure I knew that he could have let go." She didn't want to believe me. I could see the disbelief in her expression. She sat on the step alongside me, hugging her knees to herself. "It's the truth, Sheila. I wouldn't lie to you."

She gave a faint nod. "On the way back," she said. "While you were up ahead of us, Mark said…" She stopped.

"What'd he say?"

She let out a breath. "He said you'd say something like this. Said that you wouldn't like it that he'd saved you, that you'd try to make it look different than it was."

"And you believe him and not me?"

"No." The answer came too quickly. "I told him he was wrong, that you weren't like that." I could hear doubt in her voice—at least I thought I heard it. She was smiling at me, her hand on my arm. "I believe you. Of course."

"Look," I told her. "He's jealous of us. You know that already. And he's having a tough time at home. I don't know Mark right now. He's changed; he's not the same guy I grew up with. Not anymore. I'm beginning to think he might be a little dangerous, too—to me, or maybe even to you."

She looked at me strangely then. I remember that glance: mostly the eyes. Her gaze was skittish and tentative, the type of look a person has when they reach a hand out to a dog they thought they knew and it growls at them. Or maybe she was simply surprised that I'd say that when it was what she was thinking herself. Or maybe, maybe I'd startled her with a sudden truth. I don't know. "You shouldn't say that," she told me.

"Why not?" I remembered the conversation I had with him up in his room: *"When someone hurts you, you just hurt them back harder…"* "I'll tell you what I think—"

"Don't say it," she repeated, more urgently this time. She sighed, her hands fluttering like butterflies over clover. "Please don't say it, Rob. Haven't you ever been afraid that if you said what you were thinking out loud, or you thought it hard enough, it would actually come true? Something bad, something you didn't want to happen? You have to be careful what you think about. You have to be careful what you say."

I lifted a shoulder and let it fall again. "Yeah. I guess. When my dad had his appendix out, I was too little to understand what was going on. All I knew was that dad got really sick, sicker than I'd ever seen him before, and he was in the hospital and having an operation. I was afraid he was going to die, but I wouldn't let myself think that or even mention to Mom how scared I was." I shook my head. "But Dad wasn't ever in any real danger, and if I'd said something, Mom could have told me the truth and maybe I wouldn't have worried so much."

I would have said more. I know I was thinking it: I couldn't stop thinking about you after I met you, Sheila. I didn't want to move, and I thought about that a lot, too. And look what's happened...

"Sometimes people don't want the truth," she answered. "Sometimes the truth doesn't comfort you at all."

"What does that mean?"

"Nothing," she said. "Everything." She leaned over and kissed me. It was quick, her lips descended somewhere in the proximity of mine, then were gone again.

The kiss of a sister. The kiss of a friend.

"I have to go," she said. "Tell Mark I had to leave. Tell him I had to go home." With that, she got up from the porch and started walking quickly away. Toward the woods.

"Sheila!" I called after her.

I rose and she turned and shook her head at me, dark hair swaying. "I'm sorry, Rob. I need to think about things myself, okay?" She started to run, then, her feet pounding on the grass. I stood, wondering whether I should go after her, but I didn't. I watched her leave, knowing that everything had suddenly changed between us and not at all understanding why.

Mark came back about ten minutes later. "Where's Sheila?" he asked immediately.

"Had to go home," I told him.

Mark said nothing. He stared somewhere over my left shoulder, standing on the sidewalk in front of me with his hands thrust deep in the pockets of his jeans. I stared, too, past the houses across the street to the green, swaying treetops of the woods.

"Look, man," Mark said finally. "Back there, in the woods…You know I wouldn't have really let you fall. Not ever. I wouldn't ever do that to you, man. I was just fucking kidding around."

"Yeah?" I grunted. "Funny, that's not the way it felt to me."

I thought I saw true apology in his eyes, or maybe that was what I wanted to see. "I'm sorry, Rob. I don't know…" He pulled his hands from his pockets and lifted them palm up. "Well, yeah, I do know why I did it. You do too." Kitty-Kitty started yapping from behind the hedges next door; Mark grimaced at the sound, glancing that way with an angry look as he put his hands back in his pockets. "The dead should stay fucking dead," he muttered, then turned back to me. "I brought Sheila here for me, man. For *me*. You were leaving, remember? *I* was the one who needed her, not you. And now…"

That sparked the anger in me again, even as I wondered whether he really believed that. Worse, I wondered whether I did, though I wasn't willing to admit it. "You didn't 'bring Sheila here,' Mark. Her mom brought her, when they moved into their house. You didn't conjure her up, and she didn't step through your 'gateway.' She's *real*, and she's made up her own mind about who she wants to be with."

The expression on his face hardened slowly, the long muscles on his neck cording and the sympathy in his eyes draining away. "Yeah, she's real enough. I guess you know that better than anyone, huh?" he said, and spat on the grass toward the pin oak. A squirrel was sitting there on one of the low branches: a black one like those I'd seen in a trip to Toronto last year, not the usual gray ones. "There's nothing at all unusual about her. Hey, I see that you're suddenly not moving away now, and my mom, she looked at me strange when I mentioned that the sign was gone from your yard—odd how she doesn't remember a sign at all, or your folks saying anything to her about the move. Maybe I should ask your mom what happened. I wonder if she remembers anything about it…"

He started up the walk toward the house. The squirrel lifted up on its hind legs on the branch, the motion catching my eyes. The squirrel distinctly shook its head at me, chattering angrily as if trying to warn me. I stood up abruptly, blocking Mark from coming up the steps. "Yeah, that's what I thought," Mark said. His laugh was as dry as August dirt. "You're getting everything you want out of her, aren't you? Well, she was supposed to be *mine*, man." He tapped himself hard on the chest, his chin thrust out toward me, his eyes glittering. "I needed her more than you. Look at my face, look at my whole fucking family. I needed her, not you, but you stole her from me. I thought you were my friend. I thought you cared about me. About us. Now I know better, don't I? Maybe the next time I *will* let go, Rob. Maybe…"

He closed his mouth, pressing his lips tightly together as he turned and stalked away. I stared after him unable to say the words that clogged my throat. The squirrel scampered along the branch keeping pace with Mark, and finally leaping from the end of the branch to Mr. Bell's hedges. Kitty-Kitty barked. "Hey," I heard the dog say in her old-lady voice. "C'mere a minute, buddy."

Mark was already across the street and walking toward his house. I stood on my steps. Mark didn't look back at me at all as he opened the screen door and went in. "Hey," Kitty-Kitty said again through the hedge. "I'm talking to you, neighbor."

I went over to the hedge. Kitty-Kitty was sitting on Mr. Bell's perfect lawn, its long tongue hanging out as it panted. The black squirrel was laying at the dachshund's feet, the neck broken. "Why'd you do that?" I asked. Kitty-Kitty rolled her eyes, giving me a baleful look.

"I'm a dog," she said. "And that was one slow and stupid squirrel. It's instinct. Can't blame me for that."

"You didn't have to kill it."

"Don't go talking to me about choices, boy, or I'll bite your leg the next time I get a chance. Haven't you ever done something you didn't want to do because you felt you had to?" Kitty-Kitty bent her head down and sniffed once at the corpse. "I mark my territory, too. Stick your leg over here and I'll show you how it's done." The dog smiled, tongue lolling. I thought that the head appeared to be attached at a slight angle to the neck, but at least it wasn't wobbling anymore.

"I'm not your territory."

"No? You think I talk to anyone else?"

"Kitty-Kitty!" Mr. Bell appeared at his front door, opening the screen door. "Get in here!" He scowled at me.

"Gotta go," Kitty-Kitty said and barked once. "The hand that feeds me, and all that…." The dog waddled quickly away and into the house. Mr. Bell stared at me a few moments longer, then let the screen door slam shut.

I looked down at the squirrel. Its mouth was open, the head hung at an impossible angle, and blood dappled the dark fur. "It's your fault," the squirrel husked in a whispery, cartoony voice, but I didn't listen to it anymore. I didn't want to hear anything a dead squirrel had to say and I especially didn't want to see if it would get up again. One resurrection was enough.

"You're dead," I told the squirrel. "Why don't you just stay that way?"

I went into the house.

NOW, AND AGAIN

didn't go into the woods that first day back, though I wanted to. At least I thought I did. Instead, I drove down the hill from the old subdivision, feeling vaguely hungry. I decided to go to a restaurant my parents had once frequented.

The Two Century Inn was in Springdale, a few miles across the concrete river of I-75. The original structure dated from the early 1800s. Spring Pike, on which the inn was located, had once been a main road between Cincinnati (on the Ohio River), Columbus (the state capital in the middle of farmland), and Cleveland (on Lake Erie). The inn had been an overnight stopping place equipped with stables and rooms for carriages and drays, a day's journey from the Ohio in those days. A portion of that inn still existed: an ancient tavern still heated by a wood-burning stove with a few rooms above it, once used by the road-dusted travelers and now just storage.

The Two Century Inn had adapted over the decades of its existence. Its clientele had ebbed and flowed with the long years, the inn bought and sold many times over the decades. When my family had discovered it, in the year before they left town, it had been experiencing a temporary period of new popularity (which had quickly driven the price of the inn's signature fare, a fried shrimp basket with fries, from a very reasonable $3.98 to over $7.00). The clientele wandered off after a year or so, moving on to some other brief epicurean novelty and leaving the prices permanently inflated and the portions diminished, and we'd stopped going there.

At some point in the 20th century, a much newer building had wrapped itself around the tavern like a protective cloak, a restaurant that lacked the distinctive character of the old tavern. I'd never liked the addition, which suffered from terminal blandness, but the tavern section served the same food and had atmosphere in plenty, from the stove dominating the center, to the hand-hewn beams of the low ceiling, to the animal heads and hunting gear adorning the plank walls—and that was where we'd always taken a table.

I didn't know if the place was still open, or if it still served food, or if it had transformed itself into a strip mall.

It hadn't. The Inn was still there, looking much the same as it had back then. I pulled into the parking lot, frowning. There were maybe five other cars in the lot at 7:00 PM—which didn't seem to bode well. Either their dinner rush was early, or the restaurant was again in a down period. I turned off the ignition and walked toward the restaurant, skipping the entrance to the dining room and using the tavern door instead.

Two of the eight tables in the bar were occupied, and a heavyset man in a grimy John Deere ball cap straddled one of the bar stools with a half-empty beer in front of him. The TV in the corner above the bar showed the Reds being shut out by the Braves; John Deere and the bartender were arguing whether the aging Braves ace was a better pitcher than the current Reds prospect. I slid behind one of the small tables next to the window and plucked the menu from its holder—by the time I'd determined that the shrimp basket was now a hefty $10.50, a waitress had wandered over. She was no one I recognized, not that I'd had expected any of the help from decades ago to have made a career of the Two Century Inn. I ordered the shrimp basket and a draft, and started reading the articles.

The shrimp basket was neither worse nor better than I remembered, the shrimp plentiful enough though the batter was salty and a bit over-fried. I had to ask for the rye bread that used to come with the basket. I ate the shrimp, tasting more oil and batter than shrimp, and leaned back in my chair, frowning. I felt restless, I felt still hungry—but I knew now it was nothing that food could allay.

I was nearly done when I looked up toward the bar, seeing movement. I hadn't seen her come in, hadn't heard the door chime.

But she was there, standing on the end of the bar a few feet from John Deere, looking away from me with a faint smile on her face.

Sheila.

The shock of her appearance was startling. I knew that I was sitting there slack-jawed and stunned, knew that awkward seconds were passing as I searched for words in a suddenly-empty head, as I wondered whether I should stand up and wave to her. I'd planned the moment of our reunion a few thousand times over the last few months, deciding on just the right words, the way I'd look at her, at my stance…But she'd shattered all the careful strategies—the way she'd always shattered my composure.

With her presence, shadows fled in the dark tavern. I watched the waitress, my waitress, hand her a paper bag with the Inn's logo and a grease stain adorning the side. Sheila started toward the door, then turned back. Lamplight caught in her eyes.

"Sheila?" I said, half-rising in my seat.

She didn't seem to hear me. Before I could call out again, she was gone. I scooted out from behind the table and went to the door and outside, looking for her. She had vanished, impossibly. I scanned the parking lot, looking for her. "Sheila?" I called. A couple getting into their car in the parking lot looked at me. Otherwise, there was no answer.

I went inside and sat down again. I sipped the beer and nibbled on the remaining shrimp without tasting them, thinking about Sheila and how, as always, she still seemed to shroud herself in mystery. I waved to the waitress, who was talking with the bartender and John Deere. She came over to me with a ponderous, audible sigh. "The woman who came in a few minutes ago—the one with the takeout order. Do you know her?"

The waitress gave me a one-eyebrow-raised appraising glance as she shook her head. "No one's ordered any takeout."

"You just gave her a bag of food a few moments ago…"

Her head cocked decidedly. "Look, I'm the only one here. Believe me, I'd remember giving someone their takeout bag."

"Dark hair? Pale blue eyes? Interesting face?"

She just stared at me. She put the check down on the table, on a ring left by the beer glass. I watched the flimsy paper darken as it sopped up the moisture, smearing the scrawl of writing. "Pay the bartender, okay?" A few minutes later I heard her mutter something to John Deere and the bartender about how "that old guy's gotta be on drugs or senile or somethin'" with a tilt of the head back in my direction.

I paid the bill, leaving too much of a tip since the waitress, bartender, and John Deere were all watching me as if waiting to see if I'd start speaking in tongues, and left the tavern. Outside, the sun had departed, leaving the western horizon awash in red and purple, and with the evening had come the first hint of an autumn chill. At the darkening zenith, Orion swung high overhead, and the breeze held the scent of flowers. I scanned the parking lot, half-thinking that she'd still be there, that I'd find her standing alongside my car, waiting for me.

She wasn't, of course.

I drove to my motel room with a vague, ill-defined sense of disappointment.

Tomorrow, I told myself. Tomorrow I'd go back to the old neighborhood. I'd go back into the woods. And there...

I wasn't certain what I thought I might find there, but I know what I hoped.

CHAPTER THIRTEEN

I didn't see Mark or Sheila again for the rest of the day, nor the next morning. I wasn't much surprised by Mark's absence given our argument yesterday, but I'd thought that Sheila would call or come by in the morning. Mom, at breakfast, had suggested to me that I should cut the yard; I spent an hour or so pushing the mower across the grass, expecting Sheila to show up at any moment. She didn't. I was growing antsy and, yes, a bit paranoid considering her reaction to Mark's "rescue" of me, wondering if Sheila and Mark might have gone off into the woods together without me.

Which at least made me realize that—had our roles had been reversed, had Sheila attached herself to Mark rather than me—I would be as jealous of Mark as he evidently was of me.

I grabbed a peanut butter and jelly sandwich for myself for lunch, called out to Mom that I'd be back later, then headed out the back door. Most of the houses on North Crest butted up against the backyards of the South Crest houses, but down as far as we were, South Crest jogged away, allowing a small arm of the woods to come between our lot and the corresponding lot on South Crest.

I jumped the rear fence and started walking through the scrub and trash-filled patch of ground. I thought I'd go to Sheila's house and see if we could talk, maybe find out what she was feeling. She'd be there, I told myself. She'd be there…I was just about to come out onto South Crest when I heard her call my name.

"Rob…" She was leaning against a tree just past the chain-link fence of the nearest backyard. Her T-shirt said, in large ornate letters: FRODO LIVES!

"Hey, I was just on my way over to your house. I wanted to talk to you. Come on, we can sit over on your porch."

She shook her head. "No, we can't," she answered. "Not right now."

"Why? What's up?" I asked. I couldn't imagine any reason why that would be a problem, unless, like me…"Your Mom…?"

A shoulder lifted. "Yeah. Something like that." She held out her hand toward me. "Come with me. This way."

She led me back into the woods. That was fine with me. Her hand felt right clasped in mine, and I laced my fingers through hers, pressing hard. If she'd smiled back at me, the world would have been right again. But she didn't look at me at all.

She let go of my hand as soon as we were away from the houses, and went half-running along the trail, pausing to let me almost catch up, then going on again. Yet there was none of the exuberance I'd seen in her before. Her mood seemed darker and more somber, as if she were hurrying to finish a task that was distasteful to her. We moved north, toward Cooper Creek, but then she suddenly bolted away from the path, pushing through an opening in a tangle of blackberry bushes and into a tiny clearing beyond. By the time I found my way through the scratching, clinging bushes, she was already sitting in the patch of high grass. I came and sat alongside her. We were enclosed in a ring of bushes, hidden from anyone except the squirrels bounding along the branches of the trees above us. I could feel the warmth of her body down my side where our bodies touched.

I was thinking what you'd expect a sixteen-year-old boy to think.

I put my arm around her. I pulled her toward me, closing my eyes as I tilted my head for the kiss.

My lips hit cheek.

I sat back and opened my eyes. She was glaring at me, brushing at her face with the back of her hand. "That's not why I brought you here," she said.

"I know," I answered. We both knew that statement for the lie it was.

"Bullshit," she spat. "I thought you...I thought maybe you'd have known better, that you'd have understood..."

"Sheila..." I lifted my hands, let them fall again. "Look, I'm sorry. But I won't apologize for feeling the way I do about you. Being with you...that's what I want, Sheila. You know that, don't you? Or don't you feel that way about me anymore?"

She continued to stare, but the gaze softened a bit. There was a hoarse, throaty *caw* from one of the surrounding trees, and I saw a large black crow in the leaves. I wondered whether it was the same raven that had been in the circle of chestnuts, but I wasn't about to ask Sheila. It was almost cold in the clearing, an improbable chill. Even the grass looked dry and tired, as if ready for a winter's sleep. Goosebumps pimpled my arms, raising the fine hairs there. I rubbed at my arms, looking up at the sun that seemed to shed no warmth here.

If Sheila was cold, she didn't show it. She didn't seem to notice much at all. She sat with her arms around her knees, chin resting on faded, thin denim. I wanted to hold her—only that, just to hold her and give her what comfort I could with an embrace, but when I moved to put my arm around her, she lifted her head. I stopped in mid-gesture as the raven laughed harshly above me.

Sheila looked up at the creature. "Of course, that's right," she said with her face toward the bird. "But why is it never what *I* want?"

"Huh?"

She turned her head back at me as if she'd suddenly remembered that I was there. She shook her head and reached out to touch my cheek. Her fingers were warm and soft; I hadn't shaved that morning—I really only needed to shave twice a week, at most—and her fingertips snugged against the soft and erratic stubble on my chin. "I do love you," she said, her voice so soft it sounded like the wind through the trees. "I love you, Rob. That's the problem. I didn't want to feel this way, but that's what happened. And now..."

"Now what?" Her words had filled my body with warmth and heat, and I wanted to jump up and laugh. *"I do love you..."* "Sheila,

I—" She touched my lips with a finger, stopping the rest of the words before I could say them.

"Come with me," she said. "Just follow me and don't talk."

She got to her feet, brushing off the leaves and grass that clung to her jeans. I watched her stroking her rear end, wishing that were my hand. The raven lifted from its branch with a throaty cry and flapped away; Sheila followed in the same direction, as I stumbled after her, following the white gleam of her T-shirt through the yellow shafts of sun stabbing through the trees. We were, as near as I could figure, somewhere close to the chestnut circle: at least we seemed to be moving in the right direction and again—and rather impossibly given the number of years Mark and I had spent prowling this patch of forest—I didn't recognize the landscape here. We moved in a winding valley between steep hills, walking along a quickly-running stream that must be running down to Cooper Creek, somewhere off in the near distance. Sheila seemed to be looking for something, searching the hillsides around us as we walked, but then pulled me quickly off to one side.

"Wait here," she said. "I have to check something." She scrambled halfway up the hillside to our left to where a clump of boulders jutted out sidewise like gray teeth from the dirt, an oak sapling doing a tenuous balancing act above them. The raven followed her, perching on the lip of one of the boulders as Sheila stooped down, peered cautiously into the darkness under the boulders, then waved to me. I scrambled up the hillside toward her, and then crouched next to her. The smell of cool, clean earth wafted out from a hollow underneath the boulder, and with it came another smell, far more pungent and urgent. I saw eyes and heard a soft mewling. Sheila started to reach into the darkness there and I touched her arm in warning. "It's okay," she said. "They won't hurt me." Her hand came back bearing a ball of tawny fur attached to a head with tufted, pointed ears and huge, pale green eyes.

"It's a cougar cub," she said, handing it to me. "Go on. You can hold it." I took the cub. It was surprisingly light, though already bigger than any house cat I'd ever seen, and I could feel ribs poking through its skin. The cub scrabbled at my chest with sharp foreclaws for support as I cradled it, still mewling. I could feel the cub purring as I held it, a deep rumbling I half-heard and half-felt through my chest. Sheila had reached into the hollow and retrieved another cub, just as scrawny as the one I held. "Brother," she said, holding up the one in her hand, "and sister." That was with a nod to mine. "Still dependent on Mama for food, but not very well nourished." She scratched her cub behind the ears and the male stretched his neck up like a house tabby, purring loudly with his eyes half-closed. At the mention of Mama, I started looking around, half-expecting to see a huge feline form slinking through the underbrush toward us.

"A family of cougars? Sheila, there haven't been cougars around here for..." Sheila was looking at me with something approaching disappointment, her eyebrows raised. "...a long time," I finished lamely. That much was certainly true. Yes, I knew that once cougars had been among the predators in the original forests in the area, along with wolves and bears. But none of those species survived now except in the protected expanses of national parklands and the caged pens of zoos. And, apparently, here in my own woods. "How did you know these were here? If there are cougars out here, you'd think someone would have known."

"*I* knew," she answered. She put her cub back into the hole, then held out her hand for mine. The cub was reluctant to leave me; I had to pull claws out from where they'd snagged my T-shirt. She mewled piteously as I handed her over, but allowed Sheila to place her back into the boulder-hidden nest. "Come on," Sheila said again, and half-slid, half-clambered down the hillside back to the creek valley. We wandered along the creek for what seemed to be another quarter-mile or so, then Sheila stopped suddenly, crouching behind a tangle of blackberry bushes as the raven landed high up on a nearby buckeye tree; the berries—far too early—were already ripe and black and ready to be plucked: September's bounty in late June. She motioned to me and I slid down alongside her.

"There," she whispered, pointing through a gap in the bushes.

I peered toward where she was pointing, and saw a piece of brambled background ripple and move before I realized what it was: a fawn, with spots still dappling its tan coat. It was grazing on the leaves before it, a graceful creature with spindled legs and huge chocolate eyes. "Wait a moment," Sheila said to me. She rose, slowly, and the fawn's head swiveled rapidly toward her, the legs tensing as it readied to bound away. But Sheila held out her hands, making a low clucking deep in her throat, and the fawn quivered but remained still as she went up to it, still crooning, until she put her hand on the creature's neck, stroking it. It lifted its head like a dog at attention. "You can come out now, Rob," she said to me softly. "Slowly. Don't scare it." She continued to pet the fawn as I approached. The fawn startled as I came up to it, its legs flexing as it started to bound away, but Sheila whispered into its ear and it quieted. I could feel the muscles trembling in its neck as I stroked it.

"It's so beautiful," I whispered to her.

She smiled back to me over the fawn's head. "I know," she said. "Truly beautiful. And gentle." Sheila held her hand out in front of the fawn, and its long, flexible tongue licked her skin. She saw me watching. "Go on," she said.

I held my hand before the black nose of the deer. It sniffed once, and licked. The tongue was like a soft rasp, rough yet delicate. I grinned at Sheila. "You need to get a job at the zoo," I told her. "I've never seen anyone able to do things with animals the way you do. You're amazing."

She smiled again, more gently this time, and nodded with her head. "Over here," she told me, and we walked away from the fawn to the edge of the clearing. The fawn watched us for a few moments, then went back to grazing on the leaves.

I also noticed movement nearby, to the other side of the fawn's meadow: a slow and clumsy pacing masked by underbrush and saplings. Once, a head slid into sunlight, and it sparked on white and tan fur and a feline snout. A cougar—not one of the cubs, but a full-grown animal—slid forward another few inches and then hunkered down, watching the fawn. I could see that the feline was injured: its left front leg was twisted at an awkward angle, as if the leg had been severely broken and then healed in that position. When it moved again, I saw how the cougar tried to keep its weight from that leg. It didn't seem to notice us, standing nearby— I remember thinking that perhaps the breeze was from another direction. The cougar slid another few inches closer, and we could see it tensing to leap as the fawn lifted its head in sudden alarm. "No," I whispered, loudly enough that Sheila turned her head to me.

She stepped further out into the clearing. Neither the fawn nor the cougar moved; they seemed frozen in the moment of confrontation. "You have to choose," Sheila told me. "Does the fawn live or die?" She pointed to the cougar. I could see it breathing, but it still hadn't moved or acknowledged us. "That's the mother of the cubs we saw earlier. You can see why she hunts poorly. If she doesn't kill the fawn, then they go hungry and the cubs will die in the fawn's place."

I didn't question that. It felt true, somehow. I shook my head. "That's not up to me," I told her.

"It is now," Sheila insisted. "We've interfered in their lives, fawn and cougars, and now you have to make the choice. Our choices have consequences, Rob. All of them."

I stared at the tableau. Arguments raged through my head: It's just a deer, and there are dozens in the woods…But the cougars, if they live, are dangerous. They could kill a child, or they'll be noticed and hunted down to be killed or captured…Isn't it better if they just die now…?

"I can't," I told her again. "You choose."

"I already did," she told me. "I'm asking *you* to choose."

I could only shake my head. "I can't," I said. "I really can't."

With that, she came back to me. Touching my arm, she left the clearing, and I followed her reluctantly. A few strides away, I heard a growl and a high-pitched wail of alarm from the fawn. There was a commotion and a thrashing in the clearing behind us. "What happened?" I asked Sheila, looking back to the clearing, trying to see through the underbrush and intervening trees.

"You didn't choose," she told me. "So you don't get to know."

Sheila hurried back along the path we'd followed, quickly enough that we had little opportunity to talk, though I tried. "Look, I *do* know what you were trying to tell me back there…"

"Do you?" She glanced over her shoulder at me—scurrying in her graceful wake—with raised eyebrows.

"Yeah. I don't quite know how you managed to do that, but the message was obvious. I'm not—" I slipped on a wet rock at the edge of the creek and my sneakered foot plunged into cold water, sending water striders and tadpoles fleeing as I almost went down on my butt, catching myself at the last moment on a sapling growing on the creek's bank. Sheila had stopped, a grin slowly spreading over her face. "—stupid," I finished, and grimaced as I pulled my foot from the creek. "Just clumsy."

Sheila laughed, and for the first time in a while, she smiled at me the way she had before. She continued walking and I followed, my sneaker squelching wetly with each step.

We turned a corner, and I suddenly knew where we were. We stood on a hillside overlooking one of the creek valleys, and the treetops across the way were touched with that strange golden light of late day, the light Brother Wallenda, my art teacher at school, had spent hours discussing when he talked about Renaissance and Romantic landscapes.

The light that meant I was in trouble.

"It can't be that late," I said. I was looking at Sheila as if she could give me some explanation, but her face was curiously devoid of any emotion at all. I tried to think back on the day and still couldn't imagine that we'd been gone more than two hours at the most. "It has to be eight o'clock or so. Shit, I missed dinner and my folks are going to be pissed. Come on, we have to hurry."

She shook her head at me. "I'm staying out here."

"It's gonna be dark soon."

A shrug. "Stay with me, Rob," she said. "Let's spend the night in the woods." I gaped at her. She was leaning back against an oak tree, one leg bent with her Converse planted on the trunk. Her arms were back, as if she were hugging the tree in reverse. The raven was still with us also; it fluttered to a rest on a limb just above Sheila. The golden light was on her face through a gap in the leaves. She smiled, a smile that sent emotions warring inside me. "Choices," she said. The single word was crystalline in the quiet of the woods, in the gathering twilight.

"Sheila…" I couldn't get the words out; contradictory, they smashed against each other deep in my throat and fell like dust.

My hands were flailing the air. "It's gonna be bad enough now. If I stayed out all night, hell, they'd have half the neighbors and the cops out here looking for us, and when we got back..." I stopped, eyes narrowing. "Or is that something you can fix?"

"I can't *fix* anything. I would have thought you'd have figured that out by now. Our choices have consequences. Always."

I grimaced. "Then..."

"Then maybe you should go on," she told me. She was still smiling. "While there's still time." The raven laughed at me harshly from the limb above her.

"What about your Mom?"

"She knows where I am. She's not worried about me."

"Sheila..."

"Go on," she said, more gently this time. She pushed away from the tree, coming up to me and putting her arms around my waist. She pulled me to her. Her lips were warm silk on mine, her mouth opened to me for long seconds, and then she turned her head to snuggle against my shoulder.

"Why don't you come with me," I said to her. I could feel her head shake once. I wondered if she were crying; her eyes glistened when she looked up at me.

"Can't," she said. "That's *my* choice." She smiled again, letting me go. "It's okay, Rob. Really, it is. Go on before it gets dark..."

CHAPTER FOURTEEN

I could see Dad standing on the porch as I came out of the woods into our backyard. He saw me—I could see him staring in my direction. He didn't say anything, just turned and went back into the house. As I passed the Bells' house, I heard Kitty-Kitty barking in the front yard. "Hey," the dog called to me. "You're in big trouble. Maybe your parents should have you fixed. Then that bitch wouldn't get to you at all."

"Shut the fuck up," I told the dog.

"Oh, such nice language." The dachshund squatted, dropped a few black turds, then moved a few feet toward me as she scratched at the grass with her back legs, the blades flying away in the general direction of the fresh deposit. "If you didn't want me giving you advice, you should have left me dead."

"I could still arrange that," I told the dog, then saw Mr. Bell looking at me through the screen door. He scowled suspiciously and opened the door.

"Come, Kitty-Kitty," he said to the dog while watching me. Kitty-Kitty waggled her head, barked at me angrily a few times, and waddled away toward the porch.

When I went inside my house, I found both Mom and Dad sitting at the dining room table. The food was still out; the plates in front of my parents held the remnants of their meal, but there was a clean setting in front of my chair. Mom was staring at her plate as if trying to decide if she wanted another helping of mashed potatoes, but Dad was glaring at me, his lips pressed together so tightly that they were white.

I decided that a quick offensive was in order. "Sorry," I said. "I should have taken my watch with me. Hope you guys weren't too worried. Won't happen again. We just lost track of the time."

The lines on Dad's forehead creased deeper as his eyebrows lifted. "We?"

I could feel the blush creep up my neck and around to my cheeks, helpless to stop it and knowing how guilty it made me look. Worse, I *felt* guilty. Dad didn't give me a chance to reply. "When you weren't here for supper, I called over to the Dyson house and talked to Mark," he said, his voice almost a growl. "He said he hadn't been with you all day. Said that you were probably with that Sheila girl."

"Yeah. I was," I admitted.

Mom, playing with her fork, scraped the tines over the china plate with an abrupt squeal. Dad and I both looked at her, but she wouldn't look up. "Look, nothing happened, if that's what you're thinking," I said to them. "We were just walking around the woods and talking."

"Is she your girlfriend?" That was Mom. She'd lifted her head and now her gaze was on me. It was surprisingly sympathetic, I thought.

"Yeah. I guess she is."

"Well, you won't be seeing her much for a while," Dad said. He pounded his forefinger down on the Formica table hard enough that plates rattled. "As of now, you're grounded."

"Why?" I half-shouted, my anger rising to match his. "That's not fair. I didn't do anything except forget what time it was. It's not that big a deal; Mark and I have done that a hundred times and you've never been this upset. You're going to ground me for one little mistake? I said I was sorry, and it won't happen again."

"No, it won't. Because for the next few days, you won't be going outside the house. Not until your mother and I have had a chance to talk with this girl's parents."

"Her parents?" I could all too well imagine my Mom and Dad talking to Sheila's mom, and how they'd react to her. "Why do you need to do that?"

"Honey," Mom said. The smile she gave me held all the warmth of day-old toast. "If the two of you are spending so much time together, I think that we should at least meet her mother and father."

"She doesn't have a dad."

They exchanged a glance that held an "I told you so" somewhere not far below the surface. "Then we'll talk with her mother," Dad said. "We'll call her tonight."

"They don't have a phone." Their carefully-neutral expressions collapsed into tight-lipped grimaces. Dad took a long breath and his fingertips rattled along the tabletop twice. "I'm not lying," I hurried to say. "That's what the operator told me when I tried to call her myself."

Dad couldn't keep the exasperation from his voice. I could almost hear them both thinking the same thing: *This family isn't our type*...I didn't want to tell them how correct that view was. "Then we'll walk over there this evening and talk to her," Dad said. "Does Mrs. Niemann work?"

I shrugged, one-shouldered. "Dunno."

"You don't know much, do you?" Dad grated out, then sighed. "You see, Rob, that's the problem. You don't know what you're getting into. You're at an age where..." He hesitated. I thought for a second I was going to get That Talk. Dad had tried a few times before: awkwardly and poorly, but that had been a few years ago, when I'd first started sprouting body hair. "Well, you have to be very careful."

I was angry, I was embarrassed, I was annoyed at their interference in my life, I was pissed at the way my parents kept looking at each other and not at me. "Are you going to tell me about the birds and bees now, Dad? Don't waste your breath. And if I want to see Sheila, you can't stop me."

Mom gasped; Dad came half up out of his seat, his face flushed. He pointed to the door of the kitchen. "Go to your room, Rob!" he shouted. "Now!"

In the past, I would have ducked my head at that tone, knowing that I'd pushed my parents as far as I could, and I'd have headed up the stairs to my bedroom until everyone had cooled off. But not this time. I lifted my chin and crossed my arms across my chest. "What if I don't?" I asked them. "What are you going to do? Are you going to stop me from leaving if I want to? Are you going to nail the door shut and bar the window so I can't get out that way? Are you going to guard my room twenty-four hours a day?"

Dad was standing now, his hands fisted on the tabletop and his face a shade of red I'd never seen in his face before. Mom's eyes were wide and her face was pale. She licked lips that looked too dark against her skin. "Rob," she husked, and I could hear the gathering tears in her voice. "Don't do this, darling. Please. We only want to protect you, to do what's best for you."

"You don't need to protect me. You need to let me start living my own life."

Dad was glaring; Mom shook her head, the first tears glistening below her eyes. "Rob…" She sniffed, her hand going to her mouth.

"I'm not a kid anymore," I told them defiantly. "You can't keep treating me as if I am."

"You're acting like a kid right now," my Dad muttered. "You're a spoiled brat throwing a tantrum." I could see muscles twitching along his jaw line.

"Because you're talking to me like I'm still twelve," I retorted. We glared at each other. "I'm not twelve anymore. You need to trust me."

"We *did* trust you," Dad said. "We trusted that you'd be back in time for dinner. You weren't."

"You've never been late, Dad? You've never made a mistake? Do they ground you at work if you oversleep or if the traffic's bad getting there?"

"That's not the same thing, Rob, and you know it."

"No, I don't know any such thing," I told them. "I made *one mistake*, and you two are totally freaking out. I missed dinner. I'm sorry for that—but I didn't do it on purpose and it's not a big deal. I haven't done anything wrong, and there's no reason for you to punish me."

/

"You were in the woods all day alone with your girlfriend," Mom answered before Dad could retort. "You forgot the time because you were with her, and we don't know what you were doing."

"We weren't doing anything I wouldn't do here, right in front of you two," I told her, hoping that my face wouldn't flush as I told the half-lie, remembering how soft her breasts felt, or the way our tongues danced when we kissed, or the offer she'd made before I left. *"Stay with me, Rob. Let's spend the night in the woods..."* "Don't you trust me, Mom? Do you think I'm lying to you?"

I saw her glance at Dad. "We were your age once, too, Honey," she said. "We know what can happen, even if you don't really intend for it to happen. When your father and I—"

"Look, I don't want to hear this," I interrupted her quickly. I really didn't. I didn't want to hear them admit to whatever it was they might have done, didn't want to hear them try to equate their lives with mine when mine was so obviously different. Nothing in their lives could have been equivalent to what was happening in mine. Nothing.

"Well, you need to," Dad said. "We know what you're going through, son. We do. We don't want you to make a mistake that will affect the rest of your life."

"I'm not making a mistake, Dad. I know what I'm doing. Look, I forgot the time. That's all. Period. You can believe that or not, but it's the truth. I don't know what else to tell you. If you don't believe me, well, then don't believe me."

Neither of them said anything. Dad's color had returned to something closer to normal, though he was still standing. I turned and started to leave the room. "Where are you going?" Mom asked.

"To see Mark," I said without turning. "Unless I'm grounded for nothing."

There was silence behind me. I kept walking until I reached the front door, expecting to hear them say something. They didn't. I pushed open the screen door and went out.

I went over to Mark's house, angrily pushing the doorbell button. I could hear it ringing inside the house. I didn't know what I was going to say, but the frustration inside me needed some kind of outlet and I kept thinking of Mark telling my parents that I was in the woods with Sheila. I could hear the feigned innocence in his voice. "Oh no, Mr. Mullins, I haven't been with Rob all day.... No, he didn't say anything to me...Lately, well, he's always with Sheila...Yeah, I figure they're out in the woods somewhere..." I could hear him; I could see the self-satisfied little smile he would have had afterward as he hung up the phone.

No one answered the door. I rang the bell again, and again there was no answer. I scuffed my feet on their porch for a few more minutes, then left and went back home. The sun was nearly down and the shadows of the trees behind the houses laid their brooding darkness over the street.

I wondered where Sheila was in that twilight.

I wondered what would have happened if I'd stayed. But I knew I'd never know now.

CHAPTER FIFTEEN

I went over to Mark's house after I woke up the next morning. Dad had already left for work; Mom said nothing when I told her, after I finished my cereal, that I was going out. She only nodded, pressing teeth against her lower lip as if she were holding back words she wanted to say, her eyes worried and bright with moisture.

The front door opened after I rang the bell. "Where's Mark?" I asked Jackie through the screen door.

She gave a shrug at the same time I saw movement in the dim living room behind her. Mr. Dyson loomed behind Jackie in a white T-shirt, his belly a rounded shelf over zippered but unbuttoned jeans. "Who's there?" JD growled, pushing Jackie aside. "Oh, it's you, kid." He pushed the door open. I could smell coffee and cigarettes on his breath. "Come on in," he grunted.

I went in. The TV was flickering with *The Today Show*, the static-riddled face of Hugh Downs leering on the glass tube and tinny-sounding music coming from the speakers. The couch had a coverlet over it, but where JD had been sitting, I could see the rips along the seams of the cushions that the cloth was supposed to hide. A quartet of last night's beer cans surrounded an ashtray littered with crumpled butts and the crushed wrapper of a pack of Lucky Strikes. A mug of coffee steamed perilously near the edge. The carpet was hopelessly stained near the doorway and littered with Jackie's toys and various articles of clothing. Other than the television, the only light in the room came through the open front door; the rest of the windows had the shades pulled down, the draperies closed.

My Mom would have been apoplectic if I'd let someone into our house and it looked like that, but Mrs. Dyson was nowhere to be seen. I could see the doorway to the main bedroom down the hall off the living room, but the door was shut. The air in the house smelled of ancient dinners and sweat.

JD was standing next to me; Jackie had hunkered down on the floor to play with her Barbie and Ken dolls. I could feel the heat of Mr. Dyson's body and smell his aftershave. I could see the yellow stains on the armpits of his T-shirt. "Where's Mark?" he said, mockingly repeating the question I'd asked Jackie. "That's a good question, I'd say."

"If he's not here, Mr. Dyson, I'll just take off. You can tell him I came by, OK…"

His hand touched my shoulder as I turned to leave; his fingers tightened enough that I could feel them. "You don't know where he is?" JD asked. I could feel his fingernails digging into my skin. I tried to wriggle my shoulder away; he just clenched tighter.

"No, I don't," I told him as I wrenched my shoulder back with a grimace of pain. "If I knew, would I have come over here asking about him?" The corner of his lips lifted; I backed away a step. "I need to go," I added. I wasn't going to give him the satisfaction of rubbing my shoulder. I made as if I were going to walk straight to the door but JD didn't move. I had to step around him. He turned with me, watching, his arms crossed on his chest. I opened the screen and went down the steps. As I walked across the yard, finally allowing myself to massage my shoulder, I heard JD's voice from the door.

"You see him, you tell him he'd better get his goddamn butt back here or I'll hand it to him on a fucking platter." The profanities, sounding so much like Mark but spoken so matter-of-factly and loudly in the quiet air of the neighborhood, startled me enough that I could feel my eyes widen and the hair rise on the back of my neck. No one's parents ever cursed in front of the kids, not like that. I glanced back. I could see JD, holding open the screen door, one foot out on the porch. "You tell him exactly that, you hear me, boy?" he finished, and spat once on the porch steps. He stared at me for several long seconds before he stepped back into the darkness, letting the screen door close behind him.

The front door slammed shut a moment later.

* * *

I figured I knew where Mark might be. I walked across the street and past Mr. Bell's toward the wood, intending to cut between the Bell house and the house next door as we usually did. Mr. Bell was standing out by the edge of his yard, hedge-clippers in hand and Kitty-Kitty at his feet. "I know where that boy gets it from," Mr. Bell said as I approached. "Blood follows blood, I always say."

I rubbed my shoulder, now that JD couldn't see me. I figured I was going to have a bruise there. "Mark's all right," I told Mr. Bell. "He really is." Kitty-Kitty growled; I didn't dare look at her, but Mr. Bell put the clippers down and picked up the dog, cradling her in his arms. She snapped once at me, showing stained, worn teeth as Mr. Bell stroked the auburn fur between the ears. Kitty-Kitty's head, once more, didn't appear all that well-attached, moving back and forth under Mr. Bell's fingers far too much for my comfort. I half expected the head to drop onto the grass at any moment.

"I tell you that boy's heading for real trouble," Mr. Bell insisted. "I've seen how Kitty-Kitty reacts to him. Dogs know these things better than people. They can smell the rot inside." Kitty-Kitty drew her lips back from her teeth, leering at me. Mr. Bell's eyes narrowed, as if he were seeing something that pained him. "Once, that boy kicked poor Kitty-Kitty when all she did was bark at him. He'd have done worse, if I hadn't stopped him. He might've killed her."

Mr. Bell patted Kitty-Kitty's side vigorously; her head finally *did* fall off as his meaty hand slapped at her, rolling to the ground between us with its floppy ears lolling out like boneless limbs. There was no blood, no sound beyond the soft thump of the dog's skull on grass. The stump of the neck was blackened as if with clotted, old blood. Mr. Bell didn't seem to notice. He walked back to the house, and I could see Kitty-Kitty's tail wagging on the headless body as he opened the door and went in.

I look down at the head, on its side near my sneakers. One brown eye stared up at me, and the tongue came out between the teeth. "Oops," Kitty-Kitty said. "Now I'll have to lay out here until he lets my body out for my afternoon stroll. At least it's not supposed to rain."

"He won't notice?" I asked. I had a disconcerting image of Kitty-Kitty's headless body scampering around in Mr. Bell's house, bumping into the furniture and blundering into walls.

"He sees what he wants to see," Kitty-Kitty answered. "That should sound familiar to you."

"I don't do that."

"No? Well, I'm not the one conversing with a dog's head on my neighbor's lawn." As I started to walk away, Kitty-Kitty's head growled at me. "Sure, just go ahead and leave. I'm just the sacrificial victim here. Use me and forget me. Go on."

"I didn't do this to you. Mark did."

"Then you're lucky he didn't feel he needed something more significant than a lousy dog, aren't you? He sure didn't hesitate to use me." I gave an exasperated sigh and strode away, pursued by Kitty-Kitty's laughing barks. I cut between the houses and the backyards into the comfortable, familiar shade of the trees.

I took the path that led back to the Caves and the gateway. I tried to walk carefully and quietly, half-wondering if I'd find Mark and Sheila together there, and if I might hear them talking before they heard me. More than anything, I wanted to know what Sheila was thinking after yesterday, after my refusal to stay with her. I wondered if she'd really spent the night here in the woods or if she'd gone home. I wondered whether I was losing her affection, whether she might not be turning to Mark after all.

I wondered far too much. Thoughts chased themselves around my head like clouds of raucous starlings.

Mark was there; Sheila wasn't. I caught a glimpse of him through the leaves of the vines. He was standing in front of one of the gateway columns, bending over with his hands on the top stones and staring out into the woods. He looked so distraught and broken that the irritation and anger I'd been holding in dissolved. My shoulders relaxed as a tension I didn't know I'd been holding flowed away from me.

"Hey, man," I said. Mark turned his head to look at me; otherwise he didn't move.

"Where's Sheila?" he asked. "I figured she'd be with you."

I shrugged. "Haven't seen her since yesterday." He nodded and seemed to be examining the surface of the stones. "I went to your house before I came out here," I said. "Your dad...he seemed really pissed that you weren't in the house. He said..."

I hesitated, not really wanting to repeat what JD had actually said, and Mark spoke before I could rephrase it. "I don't give a damn what he said," he spat. "He can go fuck himself."

"Mark—"

"I mean it, Rob. Fuck him." He looked at me, and the raw hatred in his eyes made me step back before he blinked and smiled. "Sorry, man. Didn't mean to scare you. It's him. Just him. I've had it. I'm thinking that maybe..." He straightened. His fingertips trailed on the top of the gateway where the dark spots of Kitty-Kitty's dried blood remained. He picked at one of the flecks with his second finger until it came off, glancing once at the old blood before brushing it away on the thigh of his jeans. "Look, what I said the other day about you and Sheila..."

"Forget it," I told him, hoping I really meant that. I shrugged. He was staring at me and I couldn't look at him; I stared at the gateway instead, pretending to be absorbed in the look of the rocks there. "Just so long as you understand what's going on and you're OK with it. I mean, that bit with the vine, and what you said to me then..."

"We're cool, Rob," he told me. "Really. She's obviously chosen you—well, I can deal with that. I don't hate you for that, or her either. You gotta understand something too, though."

"What?"

"If I can take her away from you, I will, man."

"Mark, *she* made the choice, not me. I didn't take her from you. It just...happened."

"Yeah," he answered, his stare like a stone wall between us. "And so if it happens the other way, then I won't worry about you, either, the way you didn't worry about me. You understand what I'm saying?"

I wasn't sure that I did, but I nodded. Mark grinned. "That's cool, then," he said. He slapped me on the shoulder, right on the bruise his dad had raised. I tried to smile back at him.

"What's cool?" we heard Sheila's voice ask.

CHAPTER SIXTEEN

Mark and I both turned at the sound of her voice. She was standing near where we'd first seen her, her spine to the deepest part of the woods, leaning against a gnarled, stunted oak tree just beyond the gateway columns. I noticed she was wearing the same clothes she'd had on yesterday—which meant that, maybe, she really *had* been out here all night. I wondered what she'd done in the woods after I'd left her, where she'd slept or if she hadn't slept at all, whether her Mom had worried or called the police to look for her—though I knew my own parents would have first gone to Mark or Sheila's house if I'd hadn't come back, trying to find out, and if that hadn't helped, they'd have called the cops.

"What's cool?" Sheila repeated, more emphatically. She seemed to be looking at Mark more than me, but for an instant her gaze flicked over to me, and she smiled.

There was no anger nor any accusation in her gaze. I started breathing without realizing I'd been holding my breath. I smiled back at her, and her attention returned to Mark. Mark glanced at me. He grinned, the humorless and predatory grin of a shark, before he turned back to her. "Nothing special," he answered. His shoulders lifted and fell. "Rob and I were just...talking."

"About me?" Sheila asked.

"You think you're the only thing we got to talk about?"

She smiled at that, briefly, as if she saw the evasion in that. "Was it good, your boy-talk?"

"It was stuff we needed to say to each other, yeah."

"You know, if you have questions about me, you could just ask. Either one of you. 'Course, I might not answer the way you want me to." She pushed away from the oak, walking over to stand beside me. She took my hand, and I laced my fingers with hers. Mark stared at our linked hands. "So," she continued, "any other questions I can answer?"

"Yeah," Mark grunted. His gaze came up, the eyebrows like twinned storm clouds above hollow caves. "What the fuck do you see in him?"

I started to release her hand but her fingers tightened around mine. She laughed. "That's simple enough. He sees *me*."

Mark scoffed, an exhalation that sounded almost like one of Kitty-Kitty's barks. He looked away, his fingernails scratching at the bloodstains on the granite column. "And I don't?"

"No," she answered. "You don't. Not really." Then, when Mark continued to stand there, she sighed. "You only see what you want to see, Mark. There's nothing wrong with that, either, and I can understand why you're the way you are. But right now you're closed off and solid. You've put up walls around you and you only listen to yourself." She swept a hand around them as if indicating the gateway, the Seven Caves, the woods itself. "Rob...Rob doesn't have those walls. Or, if he does, they're not as formidable."

Another scoffing exhalation. "You mean he lets you be in charge of what he thinks and sees and does."

I wanted to protest. Her hand pressed mine again; I swallowed what I was going to say. Mark looked at me as if in amusement. "Yeah," Mark drawled finally. "Maybe you're right. I might have called you here, but you're not really my type. I make up my own damn mind about things."

"You didn't call me, Mark," Sheila said. "I've told you that before. I was here all along." There was a break in her voice at the end of her statement and I glanced over to see tears gathering at the corner of her eye, though she blinked to hold them back. "I don't want to hurt you, Mark. That's absolutely not what I want. I know you need friends. Like Rob. Like me, too. We're both here for you. We are. I know how you feel and I know what you're going through, and we both want to help you."

"You don't know *shit*." The last word was nearly a shout. He swept a hand through the emerald air in dismissal. He looked first at me, then her: slowly, deliberately. "I don't need you, Sheila. I wish you'd stayed wherever the hell it was you came from. All you did was tear us ap…I mean, Rob and me, we were fine until…" He stopped. He was looking at me again, at my hand in Sheila's.

He turned away.

"Mark," Sheila said to his back. She released my hand. "This is the way it has to be. It's the way it has to be for you. I love you, too. I do. You'll see. You'll understand, soon enough." She started to put her hand on his shoulder but stopped. I could see it hovering above his T-shirt, as if she were afraid to touch him. *"I love you, too…"* I kept hearing those words, trying to not feel the jealousy that burned in my gut with them.

As if he were responding to the pressure of her near-touch, he took a step forward, away from us. He stood between the two gateway columns. "Screw you," he said. "Screw you both." He laughed, as if the words amused him. "Hell, you're already doing that, aren't you? Well, I don't give a damn. I don't need you. Either of you. Never did. I can take care of myself." He was glaring at me, as if he were ignoring Sheila entirely.

And with that, he strode off through the gateway, scuffing loudly through the leaves.

"Mark!" I called after him, but Sheila came back to me.

"Hush," she said. "He won't listen to you right now. He can't."

"But…" Exasperated, I batted fists against my thighs. "He's my friend. I'm the only real friend he has."

"I know that. He knows it too, and he'll remember it when he calms down. Let him go for now." I wanted to believe her. She smiled at me, gently, and touched my face with her warm hands. "Let him go," she repeated.

I wondered if, even a few weeks ago, I would have listened to her or if I'd have gone after Mark. But I didn't go after Mark, didn't even take a step in that direction. I stayed.

* * *

But she led me back to my house, without saying anything more. Mom glanced at us from the kitchen as we came in the back door and came toward us. She glanced at my hand, clasped possessively in hers. I thought she might make some comment after the argument the other evening, but she only pressed her lips together grimly as she made the effort to smile at Sheila. "You're back early," she said to me. "Good. I'll have lunch ready in a little bit." There was too much of a pause as she turned to Sheila. "Would you care to eat with us, Sheila?"

"That would be very nice of you, Mrs. Mullins," Sheila answered. "And…" She ducked her head slightly as if embarrassed, then raised her head again to look directly at my mother. "I want to apologize for keeping Rob out too late yesterday. That was entirely my fault, and I know what I'd be thinking if I'd been in your position. I want you to know that you don't have anything to worry about. Honestly."

I saw Mom's reserve wither away. "Why, I never thought there was," Mom answered, too airily, her cheeks flushed as she smiled at Sheila. "Well, let me just get the soup on the stove…"

With that, she turned her back to us. We said very little as Mom opened the Campbell's can and fiddled at the stove. She placed the soup in front of us; I could see her hesitating as if she wanted to sit with us, then giving us a smile and going into the front room with her mug.

After we ate, Sheila and I went into the rec room. I sat on the couch; Sheila went over to the fireplace, where my guitar case was leaning against the side of the mantel. "Yours?" she asked.

"Yeah. I'm learning to play."

"Play, then," she said. She sat on the rug, cross-legged, her hands on her lap.

"I'm not very good."

"I'm not very critical. I'd like to hear what you can do. Play."

Like many teenagers, of that time and since, I harbored thoughts of making a living as a musician. I thought that if I learned a few chords, then the songs that were obviously pent up in my head would come pouring out, glistening and perfect. I didn't realize, then, that creative writing of any sort was also "work"—I thought stories, poetry, paintings, and songs were simply something that *happened* to an artist if he or she was receptive enough. My efforts to learn guitar showed that misconception; I expected the ability to play to just come to me if the fates meant me to be a musician. I wasn't much good at actually practicing, or rather, I'd work hard at it for a week, then do nothing for two. As a result, I could manage to strum a few simple chords and string them together into a song that might be vaguely recognizable if I sang along. I had a modicum of talent—that showed in the fact that I was able to play at all without having taken lessons, and that I could manage to sing mostly on key—but I hadn't acquired the persistence and dedication necessary to do much with that talent.

But I couldn't refuse Sheila. I went over to the case and un-latched it, pulling out the battered Guild semi-hollow body guitar I'd picked up and checking the tuning. "I don't know many songs," I told her.

"I don't care. Play something. Whatever you want."

I strummed an Am chord, then Em. I was running through my small repertoire of tunes in my head. I started playing "The Boxer," which I'd begun working out from the new Simon & Garfunkel record, but after a few clumsy chords, Sheila put her hands over the strings. "No," she said. "Play something of *yours*."

"I'm not much…I mean, I've just started writing some things, and…"

"Play one."

I did, unable to refuse her, with a strange combination of pride and embarrassment. The few lyrics I'd written were much the same: terribly serious, horribly maudlin, filled with self-important angst. I sang in a warbly, tentative voice caught in the crack between tenor and baritone.

> *Empty faces pass you by*
> *The strangers on the streets*
> *Mirrored glasses reflecting stares*
> *And the burning pavement's heat*

Buildings shadow wrinkled ladies
Like painted circus clowns
The sunken faces of businessmen
As gray and empty as this downtown

City scenes, city scenes
A thousand asphalt-covered dreams
City scenes, city scenes
Nothing is as it seems

"That's as far as I've gotten with that one," I told her. I was watching her face, trying to figure out what she was thinking. "I figure another couple of verses, then the bridge again, and out. You have to imagine a big drum beat behind it, and the guitar really driving hard. I can't make it sound the way I hear it in my head, just with the guitar and voice."

She nodded, and seemed to be thinking about what she wanted to say. "Where are *you* in that song?"

"What do you mean?"

"I don't hear *you* in that. I hear someone trying to be somebody else."

The criticism stung like someone slapping me in the face. I found myself wishing that I hadn't given in to her request. "I'm talking about how impersonal things are in the big cities…" I began.

"When have you been to New York or LA or even Chicago? How often do you get to downtown Cincinnati, for that matter?"

My neck burned under the collar of my T-shirt. I was clutching the neck of the Guild hard enough that I could feel the strings pressing into my skin. "Look, I know it needs some work, yeah, but…" I grimaced. "I thought you said you weren't very critical."

I could see sympathy in her eyes and that made me feel even worse. "Rob, I'm sorry. I thought you'd want me to tell you what I thought, honestly."

"I do." Once more, we both knew that for the lie it was.

"But you really only want me to say something if I actually liked it, and to be politely quiet if I didn't." She smiled.

"Yeah." I tried to smile back and only half-succeeded. "I guess. Something like that."

"I'll remember that next time." She touched my hand, and I loosened my stranglehold on the guitar's neck. "Is a musician what you want to be?"

"Maybe."

She shook her head. "There can't be a 'maybe' if you're going to do something, Rob. The people who say 'maybe' never make it, only the ones who say firmly 'this is what I want. This is what I'm going to be.' And even then there's no guarantee."

"You know this?"

She nodded. "I do."

"How?"

"Because I've already done that," she answered. "For good or ill."

"So what are you going to be?" I asked her, putting the guitar back in its case. The locks made sharp, percussive snaps around my question. "A musician? A writer? Doctor? Naturalist?" I leaned the case against the mantel again. "You're not answering."

"Maybe tomorrow, I'll tell you," she said. "In the woods. I'll meet you by the pillars." She got up, brushing hair back from her face with a hand. "I gotta go. I'll see you tomorrow. Meanwhile, write me a new song."

I told her I would, but I didn't. I tried to come up with something, but all of the words I wrote seemed tangled and inadequate, and the chords sounded too much like other people's songs.

CHAPTER SEVENTEEN

She was waiting for me as she'd promised. Without a word, she beckoned to me as I approached the pillars in the Seven Caves, leading me back further into the woods. We walked close together and slowly, my arm around her waist except when the trail forced us to go single file. "Where are we going this time?" I asked her when we were walking side by side once more. "To see the cougars?"

"You'll know when we get there," she answered. I glanced up at the sun through the trees: it seemed to be just after noon, but I wasn't wearing my watch. "Don't worry," she said. "I'm not going to keep you out here after dark again."

I looked at her. She was smiling. "You never told me what happened with you," I said. "Did your Mom give you any trouble for staying out in the woods all night?"

She laughed. It was the only answer I received. We walked on, down the hill on which the Seven Caves stood and up the next, then across its ridge and down again…and once more I found myself in a landscape I didn't know, in a new glade: here in the woods where I would have sworn, only a few months ago, I couldn't possibly have found myself lost, a place whose every last tree, hollow, and rise I thought I'd seen. I looked backward: the hill down which we had descended was certainly a familiar one, but what lay ahead was not what I remembered as being at the foot of it. I shook my head at the impossibility. "Listen," she said, stopping.

"What?" I tensed, almost crouching. I heard nothing, or, more precisely, I heard only what I would have expected to hear: the sound of the breeze moving through leaves, the faint chatter of water somewhere close by, the calls of birds in the trees, and my own breath loud in my ears.

She'd gone to a tree to one side of the glade. It was, I realized, another chestnut, perhaps forty feet tall and achingly straight before it bloomed into a spreading canopy. Sheila placed her hand on the trunk, inclining her head to the trunk, and I saw, below her hand, an ugly suppuration in the smooth bark, a dark, broken area that nearly encircled the trunk, the edges of it raised and black and rough, with orange streaks radiating out from above and below the wound. Above, looking more closely, I could see other swellings in the trunk, though most appeared to be scabbed over with bark. "Put your hand here," Sheila said. "On top of mine."

I did that, facing her. "Close your eyes," she said. "Listen..."

I closed my eyes. For a breath, I noticed nothing, but then I heard it: a basso murmuring right on the edge of my threshold of hearing, a grumbling of black earth and stone, of deep roots and water, of wind and rain and rustling leaves. There was a beat to the voice, slow and ponderous, and the murmuring rose and fell like a chant. Entwined in the song was an undercurrent of pain and suffering. I opened my eyes, startled, and saw Sheila looking at me as I pulled my hand away.

"This one lives on the edge," she said. "Halfway between the woods you know and the woods you don't. This"—she patted the ugly gash in the tree—"is what the blight does to a tree. Out here, none of her kind can escape the blight. If the wound encircles the trunk, she'll die. Look at her. See those scars above? Those are old infections that have healed, where she's fought off the blight before, years and years ago. Now she's infected again, and maybe she'll win again or maybe she won't. There are others like her, here and in other forests, living on the edge of the special places where people can still stumble across them, but there on the edge, the blight can also find them. Maybe, one day, these trees will find that the blight is gone, or they'll discover that they can beat it, and they'll drop their nuts and let new seedlings rise through the dirt, and they'll dominate the forests as they once did. Until then…" She lifted her own hand from the trunk. "Until then, there are always the secret places that only a few people can find."

I put my hand back on the tree's trunk. The song was faint, so much so that I wasn't certain that I actually heard it at all. I might have been making it all up. I might have let her convince me that I heard it. "Can you help the tree?" I asked her. "Can we do something about the blight?"

Sheila was already shaking her head. "Not out here. Not on the edge and certainly not outside it. Outside…that's not my place. I can't change anything at all out there." She stared at me. "Out there, it's *your* world and you're the only one who can change things," she said. "You know that, too, even though you don't want to admit it."

The breeze swayed the tree tops, shifting the branches above us so that the sun sparked in my eyes, making me close my eyes. I thought I could feel the ground spinning under me, and I put my hand on the chestnut's trunk to steady myself.

Singing…singing its pain…

I could feel the blighted section of the trunk, rough under my hands, and hear how it twisted and changed the melody of the tree, adding its own sour harmony, higher and discordant. Yet somehow the blight's accompaniment was part of the whole, consistent with the lower-voiced song of the tree, a counter-melody to the tree's own. The melody wasn't western or eastern or like anything any I'd heard before. There weren't words either, but I could understand that there was some underlying meaning to the song. I could see the notes: throbbing purple and rich umber where the tree's voice was untouched, and shot with motes of pumpkin orange where the blight lay just under my hand. As if I'd slipped into a waking dream, I found that I could reach into the tree, that my hands had sunk into the bark as if the chestnut's trunk was made of gelid, thick brown water. My hand sank into the yellow blight. I closed my hand on a cluster of it and it collapsed under the pressure, the motes fading and floating away under the greater current of the tree-song. I moved my hand again, brushing at where it clung to the interior channels of the trunk, and more of it faded and died. The tree-song strengthened, its melody beginning to rise and dominate.

My hand was throbbing and burning, and pressure was building up around it, as if the tree itself were squeezing me, harder and more insistent. The song was terribly loud now, throbbing inside me, making my blood dance in response, and the burning slid from my fingers up through the palm, into the wrist and my arm.

I pulled away with a shout, opening my eyes.

Sheila was watching me, a step away. I was standing beside the tree, my hand still splayed on the trunk atop the blighted section. I took my hand away. My skin was tingling and burning, and the echo of the tree's song still lingered in the throbbing of blood in my head.

The tree looked no different. No different at all.

"Trees change in years, not moments," Sheila said, as if she were listening to my thoughts.

"Did I...?"

She gave me a quick laugh. "Maybe. You'll know one day. When you come back here."

"How?"

"Because you're 'between' yourself, Rob. Because you haven't made your choice yet—whether to be in one world or the other. But you're going to have to choose, Rob. You're going to have to choose soon."

"I know what I want," I said, looking at her.

"Maybe." She smiled again. "I know you think you do right now. But it's not that easy. You forget what a choice leaves behind. You forget that you have to make choices out there as well." She nodded her head toward the familiar ridge of the hill as she spoke. She put her hand on the trunk of the chestnut, placing the fall of her hair against the bark as if she were listening to the interior song, and nodding. "The blight's wounded, and it's in pain," she said. "Whenever you heal one thing, you kill another. That's the way the worlds work, everywhere."

I shrugged. "Who cares about a stupid chestnut blight? Let it die."

"The blight cares very much whether it lives or dies." Sheila smiled at me, standing up. "I know this much: every change we make causes a dozen more, and those another dozen each, and then..." She stopped. She put her hand on my shoulder and, leaning in, kissed me softly on the mouth. "Don't look at me like that. I'm trying to help you, Rob. I love you," she said.

"I..." I hesitated. *Love.* It wasn't a word I'd used with anyone before, not in that way, and it closed my throat so hard I had to swallow. "...love you, too," I finished. She noticed the tardiness and stepped back, though there was a grin on her face, white teeth gleaming.

"Had to think about it before you answered, eh?"

"No, I..."

Her hands were on her hips now, her head tilted in challenge. "I know," she said. "You need to take the time to figure out how you feel and just saying those words scares you. That's fine. You don't have much time, but you still have a little." Then she smiled again, and came forward to kiss me again, longer this time, our mouths opening under the pressure. After a long minute, she sighed and stepped back. She started walking away as I was still opening my eyes.

"Sheila?"

She waved her hand over her shoulder without looking back. "Think about it," she said. "I'll find you later."

"Wait!" I started after her, but she only waved again.

"Later," she repeated. I wanted to run after her, but my legs wouldn't respond. I felt as firmly rooted there as the chestnut. My breath fast, my heart pounding, I stood there because I had no choice.

A few minutes later, she was lost among the trees.

CHAPTER EIGHTEEN

I came out of the woods behind Mark's house, a deliberate move. From the little hill just past the Dysons' rusting chain-link fence, I could see him sitting on the picnic table next to the detached garage. None of his family—his dad, especially—were around, so I came down the hill and hopped the fence.

There was a battered and dusty shoe box and little plastic figures out on the picnic table: toy soldiers laying in tangled, dead olive heaps on the pine landscape. It had been ages since I'd seen that box or those soldiers, but years back Mark and I had spent nearly every day with them. I had a similar box somewhere in our basement, stuffed with identical rigidly-posed infantry, the undying battalions of our imaginations. Mark had one of the soldiers in his hand, twirling it idly in his fingers as he held it up to his face, though his stare seemed to be settled somewhere well beyond the figure.

"Hey," I said.

Mark shivered, dropping the plastic soldier on the table. He lifted his chin. "Hey."

"Been a while since I've seen those," I said, sitting down across from him and picking up the soldier he'd dropped.

"Found 'em in the garage. I'd totally forgotten about them. It's been, what, four or five years or more since we've played with them?"

"We had a lot of fun with these." I pretended to shoot Mark with the soldier. *"K-pow!"* Once I would have been that soldier, at least for a moment. I would have seen smoke and flame erupt from the end of the carbine; I would have watched my enemy fall. Now I saw nothing. I could cure chestnut trees; I could talk to dead dogs; statues could talk to me in church; I could stop my parents' moving—but there was no magic here. The soldiers were lifeless, rigid plastic. Mark stared flatly at me, and I put the soldier down.

"Look, man," I said. "I hate this. I just wish we could put things back the way they were between us."

"Do it, then," he said. "Go on."

"I don't know how." I spread my hands.

"That's 'cause you don't really want to," Mark said. "That's the problem. Maybe I should go pray to that fucking statue in the church, huh? Maybe that's the only goddamn way. You know—" he stopped; we both heard the side screen door slam on his house.

"Mark, what the hell are you doing out—" I saw Mr. Dyson scowling toward the backyard. I wondered again why he was home in the middle of the afternoon. He hadn't shaved that morning, though he was wearing his company shirt. He saw me, and he swallowed whatever he was going to say to Mark; it didn't look as if it tasted good going down. "Rob," he said, nodding once at me. "I thought Mark was alone."

He came toward us, stopping at the end of the picnic table. He glared down at the soldiers. "What's this?" he grunted at Mark, pointing. "Are you playing with…" He hesitated, and I knew there was an adjective there he deleted. "…toys?" he finished. "What's with this stuff? I told you to get the garage cleaned, not fool around out here."

"Sorry, Dad," Mark said. "I found the box when I started working on the garage, that's all, and then Rob came over and—"

"I made him show me the soldiers, Mr. Dyson," I said. "Mark was in there sweeping when I came by, but I saw the old shoebox and brought the soldiers out and made him look at them with me. You remember, we used to play with 'em all the time. That's all. It's my fault, not Mark's. Really."

Mark sent me an appreciative glance, but JD wasn't looking at me at all, just staring at Mark, who returned the gaze with a hard expression I couldn't read. All I knew was that if I looked at my dad that way, I'd be getting a lecture about "attitude" and "respect."

"Sure," JD said slowly. He picked up the soldier I'd dropped. The pressure of his fingers bent the barrel of the gun and inclined the olive drab head toward the shoulder. "Rob, I need you to go home now. Mark's on garage duty and that's what he's gotta do. You understand?"

I understood. I understood that the moment I left, JD was going to whale on Mark. I could see that Mark understood it too. I fidgeted, not wanting to get up and leave because I'd be abandoning Mark. JD was still holding the soldier, pressing it, distorting it in his thick, muscular hand. I wondered what it would feel like, being crushed like that.

There was a pop, like a firecracker going off, and a tiny white flower of smoke bloomed in JD's hand. "Shit!" he said, dropping the soldier. I could hear a thin, faint scream as it fell. It hit the wooden planks with a strange, soft thud, its limbs jutting out at horrible angles.

The pile of plastic soldiers writhed like maggots around a piece of rotting meat. JD stared at them wide-eyed, shaking his wounded hand. I could see droplets of blood on his fingers, like he'd pricked his thumb and forefinger with a needle. A small voice barked commands, and there was a treble crackling, a series of miniature explosions. A pall of smoke gathered around the soldiers, and JD backed away, brushing at the front of himself and covering his face as if he were under attack by invisible bees. "Ow! Damn! What the hell…"

He fled. The screen door slammed again.

Mark barked laughter. He grinned at me. The pile of soldiers, unmoving and still now, lay between us. I could see JD in the kitchen window that overlooked the backyard, staring out at us. "Now that was a miracle," Mark said. He looked at me, appraisingly. "Come on," he said. "Fuck this. Let's go into the woods."

"Your dad…?"

"Fuck him, too," Mark answered.

For the rest of the afternoon, it was almost like the summers before. We whooped and hollered and tore along the paths. We chased each other and imaginary monsters. We pretended we were kids again, before we'd hit our teens and had to contend with the rush of hormones. We pretended that this summer and JD and Sheila had never happened to us at all.

When the sun had lowered halfway down to the shoulders of the hills, lengthening the paths of pollen-dusted gold through the trees, Mark sighed. "I guess I gotta go back," he said. "Still gotta clean out that garage."

"I know," I said. "I should be getting home soon too. Look, Mark, if you want to stay overnight at my house…I have to check with my folks, but I'm sure…"

He was already shaking his head. "Thanks, but no thanks," he said. "This was good, though."

"Yeah." I didn't know what else to say. "What about your dad?"

Mark lifted a shoulder under his dirt-stained T-shirt. "Ah, I'm pretty sure he'll have cooled off by now. S'okay."

I wasn't sure I believed him. "I'll see you tomorrow, then?"

"Yeah. Come by the house, OK?" With that, he was off, moving through the trees with that old, familiar grace and ease, westward into the sun toward his house, while I put my back to the failing light and went east so I could come up behind Mr. Bell's house or mine. As I walked, I heard a rustling in the underbrush, and Kitty-Kitty was there, loping along the path as I walked, the dog's head lolling sickeningly on her neck.

"You know you can't be there all the time. Toy soldiers aren't really going to protect him."

"What are you talking about?" I asked Kitty-Kitty.

"That bastard JD Dyson. You think little tricks like that one can keep him away from Mark forever?"

"I didn't—" I began, but Kitty-Kitty growled, stopped, and then darted away into the underbrush. "Hey, where are you going?" I called after the dog, but I heard a familiar laugh behind me.

"Hey," I called out. "Sheila. I missed you this afternoon."

"No," she answered. "Actually, you didn't miss me at all. You were out with Mark and hardly thought of me at all." She was standing in a hollow a little below me, wearing a white T-shirt with a purple oval on it—a stroke of color like a single, thick brush stroke, like the painting in her house. The crow was perched on her shoulder, its head tilted as it stared at me. "It's OK. I'm really not the jealous sort. Where you going?"

"I was heading home," I said.

"You have to be there right now?"

I looked at the sun. "Not quite yet, I guess. Pretty soon, though."

"Good," she said. "Come on."

"Where?"

Her eyebrows lifted. The crow cawed and flew up from her shoulder, dark wings flapping. It rose and banked, then dive-bombed me from above. I ducked, covering my head. "Hey!" I yelled, and I heard Sheila laugh. When I looked, she was gone. I started to call after her, but then I saw her a little further down the path, running. Her laughter trailed behind, challenging me. I ran after her, pounding down the trail that wound down toward Cooper Creek. I could hear her ahead of me, drawing me on. I pursued through the golden evening, plowing through the fronds of undergrowth, my sneakers kicking up dust and leaves. Not far from the creek, I stopped, panting. I could see the curve of Big Bend—we were near where the snake had once bitten me. Sheila wasn't in sight, but there was a flash of lightness in the gathering dusk, snared on a low tree branch near me. I went over to the branch.

I realized what it was, seeing the splash of purple, before I touched it: her T-shirt.

"Caught you!"

Arms came around me from behind, and a warm body pressed into me from behind. I turned, and Sheila stepped back. "Like what you see?" she asked.

She was clothed only in the shadows of the trees.

Despite her nudity and the challenge of her question, she seemed timid and awkward, like a child caught doing something she shouldn't have, her left arm and hand masking her breasts and her right hand hiding the fleece at the joining of her legs, like a figure in one of the paintings I'd seen in art class.

I couldn't speak, though I stared. Yes, I'd seen naked women before: in paintings, in the magazines Mark and I had found in his basement. But never in real life. Never anyone that I cared about. I licked dry lips and managed to loosen my throat. "Sheila…"

"Hush," she said, and reached out with her hand to touch my lips with a finger. I could see her breasts, the umber oval of the areola, the puckered mounds at the centers. She took my right hand, led it to her breast. Her eyes closed at the touch, both of us sucking in our breaths audibly. Her skin was soft, the curve of her breast fitting warm in the cup of my hand, and I could feel her nipple harden and rise just under my thumb. She kissed me, fiercely and hungrily, and my body responded. "Here," she said, taking my hand again, guiding it, and I felt her wetness as she inhaled with a gasp.

The blood in my body felt as if it were boiling. My pulse sang in my head so loud I couldn't hear anything else. Its hues overlaid my vision and made me dizzy.

Somewhere, somehow, we were laying down. I don't know how we got there, in a soft bed of moss-covered earth and ferns. I was on top of her, our lips never leaving each other except for the necessity of taking a breath. "Rob," she said. "I love you." She was crying; I could see the tears in her eyes. "You have to know that. It's important."

"I love you, too." There was no hesitation this time, only an urgency—honestly, I didn't think about it. I was in a world somewhere beyond thought. Her hands pulled my shirt over my head; the feel of her bare chest on mine was like nothing I'd experienced before. The shock of that contact sent the air rushing from my lungs. We kissed again, tongues plunging into wide mouths. I felt her hands on my hips, at the waistband of my jeans, pushing them down as I pushed up on my hands, as she opened to me...

I don't know what happened then. I don't know where it all changed. It was as if I were suddenly splitting in two, my mind outside my body. I wanted her. I desired her and this moment more than I'd ever wanted anything in my life. But I couldn't move. My lungs were caught in a vise and I couldn't breathe at all. The blood hammered an insistent rhythm in my temples. The world performed a slow dance around me, dappled sunlight making me blink. Sweat beaded on my forehead.

I couldn't move. My body was ready and eager, but something held me back, forbidding me from taking that final, irrevocable move. "Rob?" she asked. Her hand brushed my cheek, and I realized that I was crying too.

"I..." I couldn't speak, either. I swallowed, still hovering above her. "I...can't, Sheila. Jeez, I feel...I'm almost..." I swallowed again, forcing down the gorge that had risen in my throat. I could taste acid. My stomach jumped once and I nearly threw up.

I pushed up onto my knees, sitting back with my jeans and underwear around my ankles. She lay there, looking up at me, and the sympathy in her eyes hurt worse than anything I was feeling. "I understand," she said. "This scares me, too."

"I'm not..." I started to deny it, but I knew she was right, and that made my denial stronger. "I'm not scared. I just..." A breath. "can't...shouldn't..."

She nodded, biting her lower lip. Her eyes, those wonderful expressive eyes, were full of an understanding I didn't want. She drew her legs up and hugged them, covering herself. Standing, I pulled up and zipped up my underwear and jeans and grabbed my T-shirt. "I want to," I said. "I do. You have no idea how much. Just not now. Not here."

She nodded. "It's your choice," she said, very quietly. "It was always your choice. Mark, he..."

I misunderstood—or rather, I gave her no chance to finish her thought. I felt a surge of irrational jealousy, and my face colored. "Yeah, if you'd picked Mark, he wouldn't have wimped out on you."

"Rob, that's not what I was going to say." She stood in a single lithe motion, no longer seeming to notice or care about her nudity—like an animal. "Mark needs your help more than I do," she said. "That's what I was trying to tell you. I understand that. I do. And you're right; you can't be there for both of us. You can't be both here and out there." She was crying openly now and I misunderstood her tears as I'd misunderstood her words.

"I'm sorry," I said. I started to take a step toward her and she shook her head, dragging the back of her hand over dampened cheeks.

"No. I'm fine. I love you, Rob. I do. I promise that. If—no, when—the time comes, I'll be here for you. I will." She stood there, a vision in the golden dusk, hands clasped behind her back, the curves of her body dappled with dying sunlight, her hair a nightfall around her shoulders.

I stood there, wanting her desperately, wanting nothing more than to take back everything I'd said, to start over, to pull her to me and kiss her and touch her and lower her down to the bed of moss and this time, this time, not to stop. Not ever to stop.

I wanted that. I did.

But it's not what happened. I heard a crow caw loudly from nearby, the call coming nearer, and the hoarse cry shook me from reverie.

"I…I really gotta go," I told her.

And I left her standing naked there, half-running down the paths toward home through the lengthening shadows.

CHAPTER NINETEEN

I ran, pursued by Sheila's unclothed ghost. I ran as if I could outpace my own thoughts...

...and realized that I was nearing the edge of the woods not far from Mr. Bell's yard. That felt strange, since I knew I hadn't been running that long. It was as if the woods had shrunken and collapsed in on themselves. I could hear the lawnmowers, the cars on the streets, the occasional calls, the faint blaring of stereos and televisions. I could see the backyards and the rear of the houses filtered through the branches and leaves. I stopped, hands on knees and panting as I tried to catch my breath again. My breath was the loudest sound in the universe. When I straightened, I looked back the way I'd come, half-expecting to see Sheila there.

I saw what I'd never noticed before.

There was trash everywhere: torn paper and tissues snagged on branches and brambles; a pair of plastic bags billowing out like torn sails; the rusting skeleton of an ancient, wheelless bike wrapped in vines; an overturned tricycle with its chrome handlebars cancerous with rust and the hard rubber wheels gouged with deep nicks; close by someone's backyard fence, the dented white cube of a washing machine lay half-buried in years of dead leaves. Mockingly, a used condom lay just off the path to my right.

I wondered if all this had always been there, if I'd simply chosen not to see the garbage spilling out of the houses and yards and cars into the woods, my woods, in a slow, relentless, and ugly flood.

I reached out to one of the trees and tore off the yellow paper caught there. Brittle and old, it tore in my hand. I could see the wide, blue lines—the type of paper I'd used in grade school—and the shapes of awkward, penciled letters. "...love you still..." I read.

I crumpled up the paper and put it in my pocket.

The woods thinned as I approached Mr. Bell's backyard. There were two trees there, large soft maples, and I could hear high-pitched chattering as I approached them. Under the wide, distinctive leaves, the branches of the maples were alive with dark birds. For a moment, I was startled, thinking the birds were glossy-feathered and huge crows, but then the scale shifted, the vision breaking up as the crows shattered and fragmented, each into a dozen others. I saw that these were common starlings, dour-feathered and small. As I approached, their calls became louder and more shrill. There must have been a thousand or more of them, filling the branches of both trees. I'd seen huge flocks of starlings flying overhead as they migrated south in fall, but never in the heat of the summer and never like this. They all seemed to be staring at me, watching me with polished anthracite eyes and talking to each other, as if they were discussing me. I thought I could hear mocking, avian laughter in their voices.

"Shut up!" I roared at them, and as one they went silent and still. They stared at me, crowded together like a funeral gathering. "Get out of here!" I shouted, and a few of them flapped their wings nervously. I looked around on the ground and saw a broken baseball bat, the handle gone. I flung it at the birds, the bat whirling.

As one, they took flight as the bat crashed through the branches, the sound of their wings a surprising, fluttering roar. They came at me as one before I could react, surrounding me in a raucous cloud as I brought my arms up to shield my face. I could feel the brush of their wings, though none of them struck me directly. Then they were gone, still chattering, still chastising me with their laughter, wheeling high in the sky like a mobile thunderhead and moving off south and east, deeper into the woods. I watched until I couldn't see them anymore, my heart rate coming back down slowly. I walked out between the trees they'd been sitting in, through the few yards of high weeds in back of Mr. Bell's house and between his house and the next one down. Mr. Bell was out in his front yard as I passed, on his knees digging in his garden. I didn't see Kitty-Kitty anywhere.

"Hey, Mr. Bell," I said.

He didn't reply at first. He just stared at me with his pasty, wrinkled face, his mouth twisted in a grimace. "Kitty-Kitty's gone," he said finally, still on his knees with his trowel in his hand. "You know anything about that?"

I shook my head. "I might have heard her in the woods," I told him. Yeah, I was just talking to Kitty-Kitty about Mark and his dad, Mr. Bell. How about that?

Mr. Bell grunted. "She better not be hurt," he said. "You hear me, boy? If that dog's been hurt, I'll..." The trowel was trembling in his hand. "I'll know who to blame," he finished. He turned away from me then, jabbing the trowel angrily into the black earth.

I decided that it'd do no good to argue with him. I said nothing, but ran past him and into my house.

In the morning, yesterday evening seemed like a dream, though I'd spent the evening thinking about it and replaying everything in my head, so internally absorbed that my parents both noticed and asked several times if something were bothering me. I shook my head into their questions, grunting negatives, and went to bed as soon as I could. I lay there, thinking of Sheila and seeing her standing naked and unashamed in front of me until sleep finally came.

Dad was gone to work when I woke up; Mom was in the television room, listening to a game show. I played my guitar for a bit, trying to write a song, but everything I played seemed banal and derivative. I slammed the guitar into its case and went downstairs, poured myself cereal and ate a quick breakfast, then yelled at Mom that I was going out.

Outside, the woods beckoned, but I tried to ignore their call. I thought of just walking around the block a few times, but I went across and up the street.

As I walked up Mark's driveway, I noticed that the detached garage's door was open and I could hear raised voices inside, angry and male. I could see, behind the rust-spotted Dodge Dart that nearly filled the structure, Mark and JD standing in front of the tool bench at the rear of the building. The unshaded overhead light was on, throwing harsh light on them. I didn't want to interrupt them and have to deal with Mr. Dyson when he was angry, as I wasn't certain he'd be in control of himself well enough not to turn that rage on me. I didn't want to be the object of his curses and shouts. I certainly didn't want to be the object of anything else, either.

Yet, like a driver slowing down to look at an accident, I didn't just walk away. I stopped and pressed my back to the house, half-hidden behind one of the bushes at the side.

"…told you that I wanted this fucking place cleaned up!" JD made a wild gesture toward the tool bench. I saw Mark flinch back as JD's hand swept close to his face. "How the hell am I supposed to work in here? Huh? Tell me!"

"Dad…"

"No!" JD shouted. "I don't want none of your goddamn excuses. I've had just about enough of them."

"I just fucking got out here," Mark barked at him. I could hear his voice rising to match the volume and timbre of his dad's. "I haven't had enough goddamn time to do anything. You'd know that if you'd take a fucking second of your life to actually listen to me."

I saw the flash of pale flesh a moment before the sound. The crack of JD's palm against Mark's cheek was loud and startling. Mark's head jerked to one side at the blow, and I heard his gasp. He lifted his own hand, fisted, as if he were about to strike his father; JD caught Mark's fist in his own as Mark hesitated.

"Don't you even fucking dare," JD hissed, so quietly that I could barely hear it. "I'll beat you so hard that you'll be in the goddamn hospital for a month. You hear me? When I get done with you, you won't even recognize your own face in the mirror. I promise you."

Mark was glaring. JD let go of Mark's fist with a contemptuous look and a snort, as if he were somehow amused, as if he'd expected Mark's defiance to wither. JD's obvious scorn sparked Mark's anger even more. Mark's fist came up again and this time his arm swung and I thought he was going to hit JD, but JD must have been waiting for the movement.

Even as Mark's right hand began its arc toward him, JD blocked the blow with his left arm and punched Mark hard in the stomach with his right. The air came out of Mark with a guttural "Umphh…" and I lost sight of him for a moment behind the car. When he slowly straightened, JD slapped Mark's head again, once with the left hand, once with the right, in quick succession. The overhead light glittered from JD's high school class ring that he always wore on his right hand, and I saw blood drooling from a cut on Mark's cheek. JD bunched his fingers in Mark's T-shirt, pulling him close. Their faces were nearly touching, Mark looking frightened now while JD was flushed with rage or satisfaction or both.

He said something to Mark; this time I couldn't hear the words, only the urgent sibilance of it. He was backing Mark up to where some greasy tools had been hung on nails hammered into the plywood walls. A step away from the wall, he shoved hard, and Mark collided with the wall with a thud that shook the garage. The tools—a hammer, a pair of vise grips, assorted screwdrivers—were jostled from their nails with the force of the impact. I saw at least one of them hit Mark's head as they clattered to the garage floor with the bright sound of metal on cement. I could imagine the nail heads slamming into Mark's upper back and skull.

Mark staggered and stood round-shouldered, looking down at the floor, defeated. "Now clean this fucking place up," JD snapped at him. "Do what I told you to do." With that, he spun around and started out of the garage.

I didn't have time to move. JD stopped, glaring at where I stood behind the bushes. His mouth twisted, his eyes narrowed.

I didn't wait to see what he'd say or do.

I ran.

CHAPTER TWENTY

I f it had been today, it would have been different.

I know. I know. I keep saying that over and over, but it's true. It would have been very different. A quick call to an abuse hotline, and the child welfare folks would have rushed there in half an hour to take Mark and his sister away while the cops slapped an assault charge and an injunction order on JD. A simple call, and my life and Mark's would have been much different.

But it was *then*, not today.

It was then, and I scurried back to my house shaking and trembling with adrenalin and fear, glancing once over my shoulder. JD was standing on his driveway near the curb, hands on hips, as gloomy and threatening as a thunderhead. I hurried inside, slamming the door shut behind me like a knight dropping the portcullis of a castle in the face of the enemy.

Dad wouldn't be home for hours yet. Mom was in the kitchen, stirring a pot on the stove. I could smell the astringent, sharp odor of tomato soup. "Hungry, Rob?" she asked. "It'll be ready in a moment."

If she'd looked at me, I'm sure she'd have noticed that something was wrong. She didn't. She stirred the soup, humming softly to herself to a Beatles song playing on the transistor FM radio on the counter. *"Let it be..."*

"Mom..."

"What, darling?" She turned then, finally, and her smile faded slowly as she took in my appearance. "Is something wrong? I thought you were going over to Mark's…"

"I did. Mark and Mr. Dyson…they were arguing. Mom, I think…No, I saw it. I saw it happen. Mr. Dyson hit Mark, Mom. Hit him hard, and he hit him more than once. Mark was bleeding."

Mom's lips pressed together. The stirring spoon dripped red on the floor; she didn't notice. "Your father and I have been worried about this for some time," she said. "The way he yells at them, and poor Mrs. Dyson, too…" She seemed to realize that she was still holding the stirring spoon and turned back to the stove. She whisked the soup noisily. The song ended and a commercial began. "When…when your father gets home, he and I will talk about it. Someone needs to talk to Mr. Dyson. In the meantime, dear, I don't think you should go over there."

"Mom…" *Mr. Dyson saw me, Mom. I think he'll do the same thing to me if he gets a chance.* I wanted to blurt out my fear, but she tapped the spoon against the pot and shook her head before I could form the words.

"No, Rob," she said. "I know how good a friend Mark is, but you can't do anything for him. Not right now. I'll call your father. Right now. I'll leave a message with his secretary and he'll get back to me right away. I want you to stay away from that house until I have a chance to talk with him and we decide what to do about this. Do you understand?"

I could hear the fear in her voice too, and I realized then that JD probably frightened her as well, that even as an adult she wouldn't feel comfortable going over to his house and confronting him alone, that if I told her exactly what I'd seen and how serious the confrontation had been I'd force actions on her and my father that they almost certainly didn't want to take. By the way she firmly refused to look at me and the fury with which she stirred the soup, I suspected such a situation was one that my parents had already discussed.

She was scared. I *knew* scared; I knew it very well. "Yeah," I told her. "I understand."

"Good." She turned to me then, with a smile as sincere and fixed as that on a concrete cherub. "Well, the soup's ready. Let's eat..."

She ladled tomato soup into the bowls she'd placed on the kitchen table. The soup drooled into the bowls like thick, too-red blood, like the line I'd seen on Mark's face. "I don't think I'm hungry, Mom. I'm...I'm going for a walk in the woods, 'kay?"

"You stay away from the Dysons', you hear?"

"I hear," I told her.

I pushed through the back screen door and onto the porch, striding quickly toward the back fence where I could cut through Mr. Bell's yard and into the woods. I expected to hear Mom holler after me and I wondered what I'd do if she told me to come back, but she said nothing. I could see her at the screen door, watching me as I jumped the fence.

For the first time, the cool, green breath of the woods couldn't calm or soothe me. There was no magic here; somehow, it had vanished. I saw—again—the trash behind the houses as I entered, and I hurried past the litter. I wandered the paths Mark and I had traversed so many times, and they were both smaller and shorter than I remembered. Each step seemed to bring back memories of the time we'd spent here, but there was no solace in remembrance. All those images seemed to be sepia-toned photographs from long ago, in another life, in another person's life. I hoped that Mark might show up; I hoped that I'd hear Sheila's bright voice call to me from behind one of the trees. I wanted—I *needed*—to talk to one of them. I went to the Seven Caves, but neither of them were there in the vine-roofed tangle. I tried to find the path to the glade of the chestnuts and once again failed.

Hell, I'd have settled for Kitty-Kitty's wobbly-headed presence.

If there was a supernatural energy in the woods, if I'd ever believed that I could control it, this time it failed me. Walking among the trees was no better than sitting in my room or walking the street. The mystery had receded or hidden itself from me; the woods left me alone. I couldn't feel the spell beneath the trees.

Maybe I'd made an unconscious choice already. I hoped not, because the place that choice left me was desolate and barren.

I found myself near South Crest, close to Sheila's house. I came out of the woods there. Maybe, I thought, if Sheila wasn't in the woods, she'd be home. I wanted to talk to her, to tell her what I'd seen, to see if she could tell me what I needed to do.

I came up the trail the South Crest kids had worn into the ground under the trees, following it toward the dead-end of the street and the lot where Sheila's house stood. I could hear the noise of the neighborhood—young kids screaming laughter as they chased each other in a game of tag—and see the houses (and the garbage that drifted from their yards into the woods).

I stopped. I wasn't more than twenty yards from the little circle turnaround that marked the end of South Crest. I should have been staring at the back of Sheila's small home, but I wasn't. I could see her neighbor's house, but the lot on which their house had stood was vacant, the trail I was following moving through what I would have sworn had been their yard all the way to the street, bounded by chest-high weeds.

Stunned, I gaped at the sight. Two kids ran from the end of the street onto the trail and past me, yelling at each other. I started to stop them, to ask what had happened to the house that had been here, but I couldn't. I watched them go.

"Sheila..." I spoke her name like an incantation, like a prayer. There was no answer. The seed-laden tops of the weeds swayed in the breeze, brushing me like soft, consoling hands. But there was no solace in the embrace. The house was there in my memory; I could see it. I remembered the way it looked, the way it had smelled inside. I knew the reality of it.

It wasn't there. It wasn't there at all. The end of South Crest grinned at me, gap-toothed.

I don't know how long I stared at the vacant lot. The kids ran back past me toward the street again and shook me awake once more. I turned my back on South Crest and went back into the woods.

I wandered there for a long time, trying to decide what to do.

If Sheila was gone, then I only had Mark.

Only Mark.

CHAPTER TWENTY-ONE

From the cover of the woods, I could hear a lawnmower sputtering in Mark's yard. I slid closer through the underbrush, listening to the mower's harsh song as it zig-zagged back and forth over the grass. As I approached, the timbre of the engine changed, becoming higher-pitched and louder. I knew that the person cutting the lawn had moved into the backyard of the house, where the woods crept up close to the chain-link fence. There was a little knoll just beyond Mark's fence, and I came out of the trees there, maybe thirty yards from the fence and overlooking a small grassy meadow, expecting to look down and see Mark pushing the mower. I had my hand raised to wave at Mark.

But it wasn't Mark. It was Jason Dyson. JD.

He saw me before I could skitter back under the shadow of the trees. He straightened and stopped: still holding the mower's handle, the motor roaring throatily and spewing out blue-white exhaust through the rusted muffler—the Dyson lawnmower was ancient, and burned oil so badly it often left a slight haze in the neighborhood on still summer evenings. I could see JD staring at me, his gaze almost as hot as the shattered muffler on the mower's engine. I stood there, staring back at him, feeling the rage in me working again just from the sight of him. He wiped sweat from his brow with the back of his arm. Seeing him, I started to really worry about Mark, because Mr. Dyson rarely mowed his own lawn, especially in the heat of summer. He always, *always*, gave that task to Mark or even, sometimes, Mrs. Dyson. If JD was out there cutting the grass, then maybe Mark was too hurt to do that job.

I wondered if I was the cause of that. Maybe JD had been so angry after realizing that I'd seen him beating up Mark that he'd gone back to finish the job he'd started. Maybe I'd caused Mark to be hurt even worse than he would have been otherwise.

Mr. Dyson stared; I stared back. The mower grumbled, missing as it idled, and Mr. Dyson slapped at the throttle bar. The motor died in a final cough and a vomiting of blue exhaust. I blinked: the silence was almost a physical blow.

"Come here, Rob," Mr. Dyson called out into the terribly still air, gesturing to me. "I want to talk to you."

I shook my head, mute.

"I said to get the hell down here, boy," he called out, more loudly this time, his face flushed with heat or rage or both. "Now do it."

I shook my head again. The anger and fear of him was molten in my stomach. I pointed at him. "I saw you," I called down the hill. "I saw what you did to Mark. I saw you hit him. You think I'm stupid enough to let you do that to me?"

"Fuck," he said low but distinctly, and he abandoned the mower to sprint toward the fence. The movement startled me; I'd rarely seen an adult actually run. When he put his hands on the top bar of the chain-link and jumped the fence, my heart hammered hard against my ribs and I came out of my stasis. He was already thrashing through the high weeds up the slope toward me; I turned and fled into the woods, into their welcome fragrance and emerald twilight.

I had the advantage of knowing the ground far better than Mr. Dyson, and of being younger and in better shape. I'd seen what he could do to Mark, who was decidedly stronger than me, and that memory lent me speed and endurance as well. I figured that as long as I stayed ahead of him, I'd be fine. I knew the woods; I had a good head start. I could lose him in the labyrinth of the trees, then head home at my leisure. He wouldn't dare follow me there, and Dad might be home by then, or Mom would call the cops if I told her JD was chasing me. I started heading west and south, toward the Seven Caves, not staying to the paths in the woods but cutting across them. Well behind, I could hear Mr. Dyson bulling his way after me. Under the shade now, away from the houses, he bellowed in rage: "Rob! You'd better fucking stop! If you don't, I'll give you worse than I gave Mark! You hear me, boy! You fucking *stop*!"

The fury in his voice powered my legs. I flew through the forest, almost as quickly as Mark usually did, if not with his grace and quiet. As Mr. Dyson continued to shout and holler behind me, I ran.

I don't know how long I fled. I turned north to go deeper into the woods, thinking maybe Mr. Dyson would think I was heading toward Cooper Creek, then looped back up toward the Seven Caves. By the time I reached the "gateway" where we'd first seen Sheila, panting and out of breath, I realized that I hadn't heard Mr. Dyson for some time. Trying to calm myself, I leaned against the stones there, hands on knees. I listened…

I could hear the leaves of the canopy brushing each other in the breeze that would never be felt down below, and at my feet diamonds of sun-shadow winked in the loam. Beyond the gateway a mourning dove hooted. I couldn't hear anything from the neighborhood at all: not a lawnmower, not the hush of tires of asphalt, not the kids playing in their backyards. I was alone.

No. Not alone.

I heard the rustle of fallen leaves, crackling like dry fire, from just beyond the stones, and a shaking of vine-bound branches above me. I jumped.

Kitty-Kitty padded out from the underbrush as a huge crow settled itself in the branches above the gateway. In the dog's mouth were a white T-shirt and a pair of jeans, the tightly-rolled bundle looking ludicrously large and clumsy in the dachshund's tiny mouth. The dog dropped the clothing at the foot of the nearest column with a yap of relief. The crow cawed once. "You'll need these," the dog said, looking at me.

I'd thought—somehow—that those were Sheila's clothes, but I recognized the frayed right knee on the dog-saliva-marked pant leg. "Those are *my* clothes."

"Well, they certainly aren't mine," Kitty-Kitty answered. "Frankly, I never understood why you people bother. Clothes just get in the way of peeing, shitting, and screwing."

I didn't have a good response for that. I stared at the clothes, at Kitty-Kitty, at the crow. "How…" I started, but Kitty-Kitty barked and shook her head, which waggled dangerously.

"How I got them isn't important. You'll need them; I brought them. I shouldn't have, all things considering, but you've at least tried."

"Tried *what*? Why will I need the clothes? Look, have you seen Sheila…?"

But Kitty-Kitty was no longer listening to me. The dog whined, crouching down with her tail tucked. She slunk away behind the stones, though the crow stayed where it was, glossy feathers sparking blue as its head turned. I followed its dark gaze. Behind me, I heard a loud thrashing and a curse.

"Don't you *dare!*" JD roared at me as I spun around and started to flee again. He was standing at the vine-draped entrance to the caves. I could see a long rip in his Bengals T-shirt where a branch or thorn had snagged it, the frayed edges bloody from a deep scratch underneath. He was panting, his face dark with blood, and his eyes were wide and burning. He pointed a thick finger at me. "Don't you dare run, boy. Don't you move."

I should have ignored him. I should have taken off once more. I could have lost him fairly easily, as I'd done before. But this was my place, my woods, and here he was the intruder. I felt comfortable here, I suppose. Safe. I could always run if I needed to. So I stayed, crossing my arms as his chest heaved and he held onto an oak sapling for support. "I saw you," I told him again. "I saw you beating up on Mark. Nothing you can say changes that."

His eyes narrowed. He shook his head: once, twice. "He's my son. That gives me rights. And after what he said to me…He deserved what he got."

"Mark's just a kid."

JD gave a laugh that was mostly a cough. "A kid? Not anymore. He's damn near as big as I am. And if he's gonna mouth off like an adult, then he can goddamn take his beating like one, too." Then JD's voice changed, and his face as well. All the anger in him seemed to collapse, like flaming logs falling in under their own weight.

"Shit," he said. His gaze went around the area as if he were searching for something. "This wasn't what I wanted. This was never what I wanted." The skin of his face sagged, like a bolt of human-featured cloth draped over his skull. His left hand, clenched in a fist at his side, opened as a quick, pale flower. He took in a long breath that shuddered in what I thought might have been a sob. When his eyes finally found mine, it was as if a scrim had been lifted from them. Clear, they regarded me. "Rob...I don't want to hurt Mark. I really don't. You gotta understand. It's just..."

He pushed himself upright. He took a step toward me, his hands held out in supplication. The crow cawed in the tree, but he didn't even look at it. He sniffed. "You don't know what it's like, Rob, to feel so fucking trapped. Hell, when I was your age..." He took another step, shaking his head. One side of his mouth lifted and dropped again. "I had such incredible dreams: all the places I was going to see, the things I was going to do, the people I was going to meet. College—I was going to go to college, somewhere far away from here. I wanted to study archeology; can you fucking believe that?" He cough-laughed again. His chest heaved. "Archeology. I'd read stuff about King Tut and imagined that I'd find something like that one day. I'd be famous. Me. I'd *be* someone. Everyone would know me."

Another step. He was close enough now that I could see the bloodshot veins in his eyes and smell his sweat. "I saw a few lousy movies and read a few books, and got this romantic vision in my head: me digging in some Egyptian ruins, or maybe in the jungles of India or Africa. Hell of an image, ain't it? Fucking pith helmet and everything." Bitterness pressed his lips together, and he was staring past me, staring over my left shoulder so hard that I wanted to turn and look myself. "You know what happened? I never went to fucking college. Never got out of this damn city. Never got none of what I had in my head or in the books or the movies. Even what little bit I did get turned sour. I got a wife I can't even stand to look at, got a kid who thinks he's fucking superior and looks at me like he's looking down on some poor pitiful dog, and another one who's going to be a useless, empty mouse just like her mom. And I don't even know how I got here, or why I stayed here so long, or how or when all those great dreams I had managed to just fucking evaporate."

"Mr. Dyson...JD..."

His gaze snapped back to me then, and the hardness was back in his eyes. The crow cawed alarm and I heard it flutter up. JD's left hand flashed and caught in the chest of my shirt, the cloth bunched in his fist. "But what I got is *mine* and it's gonna stay mine. I get to do with it what I want, and I ain't letting you interfere. I ain't letting anyone interfere."

His fist hit me in the instant after I saw it in my peripheral vision, as I pulled away against the grasp he had on my shirt: a roundhouse blow with his right hand that hit me flush on the side of the face. The pain exploded behind my eyes in fireworks of bright reds and yellows. I was on the ground, I realized suddenly, and my mouth tasted of salt and copper. JD was standing over me as I spat blood and rolled slightly in the leaves to look up at him, bringing my hand to my throbbing jaw while I opened and closed it once, wincing.

I wanted something to happen. I wanted the magic. I willed the vines to come down from the trees and snare themselves around JD. I imagined the cougar mother bounding into the clearing to leap on him.

Nothing happened.

JD glared down at me. His fists were balled at his waist. "I ain't letting you interfere, either," he grunted. "You hear me? You say anything, *anything*, about me to your parents or the cops and I'll find you afterward. You understand me, boy? I'll find you afterward and I'll make you pay. Answer me, goddamn it. You understand me?"

I saw him draw back his foot. I knew he was going to kick me. Afterward, I could imagine JD being repentant and sorrowful, scared and horrified by what he'd done...but right now there was nothing but rage in his eyes and I knew I was his target. The crow came down, dive-bombing toward JD's head so that he looked away from me for a moment.

There was a stout limb on the ground, close to my right hand. I didn't think. I don't believe at that moment I was even capable of thinking. I was only reacting, protecting myself as any person would, as any animal would. With a shout, I grasped the stick and swung it low and one-handed. It hit JD in the side of his knee and he howled, limping back a step as I rose. The crow had landed on the granite stone of the gateway. Whatever control or rationality there might have been in JD was shuttered behind the hard shells of his eyes, as expressionless as the eyes of the crow. "You goddamn son of a bitch!" he shouted at me. "Now I'll fucking kill you!"

He threw another roundhouse punch at me, wildly, and at the same time I swung the stick again. His knee went out with his punch, turning him so the stick caught him square in the nose. Blood spurted, a spray that splashed on the stick and me, that spread a fan of blood over his cheeks. He went down hard and sideways.

I heard his head hit the polished granite of the gateway column even as the crow flew up and away: the waist-high column where Mark had once chopped off Kitty-Kitty's head. JD's skull struck the rocks with a terrible sound, the sound you'd hear if you dropped a ripe cantaloupe on a concrete porch step. He crumpled to the leaves. I could see more blood spattered on the stones. My jaw throbbing, I stood over him, my own rage evaporating in a new fear. JD's eyes were open but they were looking at the ground somewhere beyond me. I don't know what he was seeing. His fingers twitched, his legs thrashed wildly. Then, horribly, they went still.

The crow landed again on the gateway, eyes like ebon rosary beads watching me.

I stood there just breathing. JD lay without moving. He never said anything and his eyes were still open even after I dropped the stick and sank to the ground alongside him. "Mr. Dyson? JD?"

He didn't answer. Couldn't answer.

There was too much blood, on him and on me. The only breathing I could hear when I pressed my head against his chest was my own, and that was so loud that it drowned out the world.

The crow flapped away into the woods.

CHAPTER TWENTY-TWO

"Rob?"

I heard her, but I couldn't move. Couldn't answer even though I heard her sobbing.

"Rob?" Her hand touched my shoulder and I started as if waking up from a nightmare.

But the nightmare was still there before me. I knew it wasn't going to go away, no matter how much I wished it would. Sheila's hands pulled at my arms; I let them lift me up. My legs ached; I don't know how long I'd been kneeling there, staring at what I'd done, staring into dead eyes that would never look back.

"I...I..." The words wouldn't come. "...didn't mean...didn't want this..."

"I know," Sheila told me. "I know." She was crying with me, letting me sob my fear and horror into her shoulder, hugging me as I tried to breathe in great, gulping gasps, as I tried to imagine away the horrible memory, as I tried to believe that any moment now I'd wake up in bed, that I hadn't just done what I'd done.

"We have to hurry," she said finally. "We have a lot to do."

"What?" I asked her. "What can we possibly do?" I glanced back at the body. JD was still there, staring blindly into rotting leaves. "Jesus, Sheila. I killed him. I killed..." I stopped. The gorge rose in my throat, and I was quickly and noisily sick. I wiped my mouth with the back of my hand, tasting blood and vomit. "I have to go back home. Mom and Dad—Christ, how am I going to *tell* them, Sheila? How? And the police...God, I can't believe this..." I was physically shaking now, the full import of what I'd done pressing down on me, the shock making my skin cold. I kept wanting to pretend that none of it was real, but the body remained there, an accusation. I clutched at my hands to keep them still. "He was going to hurt me. I had to do it. He didn't give me a choice."

"I know," Sheila said again. "It wasn't your fault, Rob."

I wanted to believe that, and the sympathy in her eyes told me that I could. "They'll believe me, too…the police…" But she was shaking her head, her hands soft on my face.

"No," she told me. "They won't."

"They *have* to," I insisted. "It's the truth."

"How many times did you hit him with that stick? And how many times did he hit you? Once? You have a bruised jaw, that's all." She took my head in her hands and gently, gently forced me to look down at Mr. Dyson. "Smashed nose, cracked skull, his knee-cap shattered, bruises on his body, probably cracked ribs…Are they going to think that was self-defense, Rob? Is that what they're going to believe?"

"But it's true," I said.

"I know that. But they won't believe it. They won't."

"Mark will tell them. He'll tell them how he was."

"Maybe," she said. "Maybe he will. Or maybe he's just going to see that you're the person who killed his father. Maybe he's going to be angry that you did what he wanted to do and couldn't. But even if he does tell them everything that happened, he's still just a kid defending his friend and he wasn't here to witness any of this, was he? No one was here but you and that awful man, and all the police will consider is the evidence that they see here."

I thought I was going to be sick again as she spoke. The woods were dancing drunkenly around me, the trees tilting one way, then another. I couldn't catch my breath, couldn't pull in any air. A panicked, wild terror threatened to take me and send me screaming. I wanted to sink back down because my legs were threatening not to support me. "Rob…" Sheila's voice was the only steady point in my universe. I clung to it. "We can take care of this. You and me. Together. We can take care of this."

"How? Oh my God, Sheila…"

"We can take care of this," she repeated. "You have to trust me. Just…"

"Just what?"

She didn't answer me directly. She licked her lips, her gaze more serious than I'd ever seen it. "Choices, remember? You have to understand that if we get rid of this, Rob, it changes everything. You'll have to leave; if you stay here, everything you've done will unravel. It will all fall apart. We can make this go away. We can make this so no one will ever know what happened here. But that will end everything else you've put together. It has to."

"Why? What are you talking about? I don't understand."

"Mark will be asking questions, and so will the authorities, and you know…" She stopped. She touched my cheek again. "You know that any questions about me will be awfully hard to answer, won't they?"

I wanted to deny it. But I looked at her and I knew I couldn't.

"Things have to go back to the way they were. Before me. You have to go to Pittsburgh," she told me again. "And I have to stay here. That's the price."

"Sheila…"

"There's always a price," she answered before I could frame the question. "For everything. And neither of us want to pay the price for *this*." She pointed at Mr. Dyson. "Do we, Rob?"

I shook my head, mute.

Sheila took a step back from me, and she was suddenly cold and very adult. The crow fluttered above her, and Kitty-Kitty emerged out from the underbrush. Sheila looked at the crow. "I know," she said. "It's my fault. It's because of my choice." She took a breath and turned back to me. "All right," she said. "Let's get started…"

Sheila walked me down to the creek; there, she made a poultice of mud and creek water and some herbs and grass she gathered, and put it on the side of my face where JD had hit me. "This will take the swelling down," she said, "and stop the bruising from showing. We can't have anyone noticing that, can we? If you show up with a bruise, there will be awkward questions that you wouldn't be able to explain away." Then she told me to stay there and hold the poultice in place, and left for a bit.

Kitty-Kitty sat on her haunches next to me. The crow settled in a buckeye tree across the creek. The creek gurgled with incongruous, bright laughter. "You know, I bit the bastard once," Kitty-Kitty said. "It was a couple of years ago, when he passed our yard and Old Man Bell accidentally left the gate open. JD tried to kick me afterward, but he missed. Howled louder than a bitch in heat. Kinda makes me wish I hadn't been given those rabies shots. I hope the bites got infected. Bastard." I didn't say anything, and the dachshund put her head on my leg. I reached down to scratch the ears. There didn't seem to be any bones connecting the neck to the body; I took my hand away, afraid the head might roll free again. "You did the right thing," Kitty-Kitty told me. "Hell, you may have saved Mark's life with this."

I wanted to believe her.

When Sheila came back, she had two rusty shovels, a bucket, some towels, and a green tarpaulin. She handed the shovels to me; we filled the bucket with creek water and went back up to the seven caves. First, we scrubbed the stones with water from the bucket and the towels until the bloodstains were gone. "They'll still know," I said. "We've got the ground all wet here, and if they look..."

She shook her head. "It's going to rain tonight. Hard. Just a few hours from now. That will cover what we just did and take care of anything we've missed." She tossed the towels into the bucket.

We rolled JD onto the tarpaulin, put the bucket on the tarp with him, then used it to drag him near a small depression about thirty yards from the gateway. There were a few young maple trees growing in the muddy ground there, finger-thin trunks rising to about my height. "We're going to dig these up, roots and all, and take them out," Sheila told me. "Underneath, the ground will be soft."

I nodded. After my initial panic, I was feeling nothing at all, and the numbness was more frightening than the fear. I dug, following Sheila's directions, not talking to her, not thinking, not daring to look at the body on the tarp behind us because I might see JD glaring at me accusingly. We dug a shallow grave, barely long and wide enough to hold the body and maybe four feet deep. By the time we finished, I was sweating profusely.

We tugged and pulled JD's body over to it and let it fall in, tarp and all. Sheila tossed in the bucket and towels. Kitty-Kitty padded up to us, the rolled-up jeans and T-shirt she'd brought me again in her mouth. Her head looked as if it would fall off at any moment, and her fur was patchy and scabrous. She looked ill and half-dead, as if she could barely walk. The dachshund dropped her burden at my feet. Her bark sounded more like an asthmatic cough. "Now those bloody clothes," Sheila said. "Strip."

I stared at her. The expression on her face might have been a smile. She turned her back. "Go on. Do it," she said.

I did, quickly. "When they find the grave," I told her as I pulled up the jeans Kitty-Kitty had brought and slipped on my sneakers, "they'll figure out these are my clothes."

"They aren't ever going to find the grave," she insisted.

"I'll still be muddy when I get home…"

"How often have you come out of the woods muddy?" she answered. "That's nothing unusual. Your parents won't even notice, won't even think about it. Just start filling in the hole."

I did, shoveling the dirt onto Mark's dad and listening to the sad, final sound. After we'd covered the body with a good foot of earth, Sheila retrieved the maples we'd set aside and placed them carefully on the earth above the body, packing them down so they stood upright as I shoveled more dirt into the grave. "Good food for the trees," she said to me. "They'll grow fast, big, and healthy. Their roots will hold earth and bone. They'll hold secrets."

The way she said it, as if she were speaking an incantation, made me shudder.

When we finished, the depression was no longer a hollow but was level with the rest of the area. We spread the remaining dirt around, spread leaves and mulch and branches over the newly-turned earth and the marks we'd made dragging the body. When we finished, when I looked at what we'd done, I could almost believe that it would work. The saplings looked as if they'd grown there undisturbed for a year or more.

"It will work," she told me as if she'd heard my thoughts. "I promise you that much. They'll never know. I'll be here to make sure of it." She looked at me. The crow had vanished and Kitty-Kitty was nowhere to be seen. "But you'll know, Rob. You'll always know. That you'll have to take with you, and I can't do anything about that. Now...you have to go."

"Sheila..." I started to go to her: to hug her, to kiss her. But she took a step back, shaking her head.

"It's too late for that," she said. "It's done. You go; I stay. Remember? That's the price, and it's already been paid. Already done. You'll see."

"Sheila, we can still—"

"No, we can't, Rob," she interrupted. "Not now. Not yet. Maybe never."

"I...I love you, Sheila. I do. I know that now."

The crow laughed. Sheila caught her upper lip in her teeth, looking away. "I know you do," she told me finally. "And if you find that doesn't ever go away, then come back for me, Rob—not in a year, not in two, not five. Later. You'll know when. Just..." She stopped. She gave a sigh that was wrapped around a sob. "Come back for me when you can. I'll be here. I'll always be here."

With that, she stepped back again, still looking at me. A step, another...and then she turned. I watched her go, watched her slide deeper into the woods until I could no longer see her.

I shivered. I looked at the two maples above the hidden grave.

I ran the other way.

CHAPTER TWENTY-THREE

I came out of the woods just down a bit from the Bell house, cut through the backyard there and started up the sidewalk toward home. My thoughts were whirling in my head, confused and uncertain. Clouds were gathering in the west, hiding the sun and promising a thunderstorm. Cars drove past me, driven by neighbors who waved. I waved back, trying to pretend nonchalance. I could hear kids playing in the yards and the throaty chorus of lawnmowers trying to beat the rain.

I didn't hear a lawnmower at the Dyson house, though.

The neighborhood seemed ordinary. For a moment, just a moment, I could almost believe that I'd walked out of some awful, horrible nightmare and back into normalcy. Then I saw the mud drying on my pants, and when I opened my mouth, my jaw ached from where JD had struck me. My tongue pushed on teeth that were loose in the gums.

Mr. Bell was out in his yard, on his knees next to the narrow band of garden behind the fence. He was patting the earth around a flower, next to a small white cross I'd never seen there before. Metal glinted from the buckle of a small leather band placed over the cross. Tags hung from a ring next to the buckle.

A dog's collar. I could read the name painted in crude black letters on the cross beam. I felt my stomach churn.

Mr. Bell was glaring at me as I walked past. "When I find the son of a bitch who killed my dog, I'll kill him myself," he said, just loudly enough that I could hear him. "You tell 'em that, boy. Tell 'em that for me."

I said nothing, but I nodded to him and he nodded back as if satisfied. I hurried past Mr. Bell into our yard.

And stopped. The sign was back in the yard. FOR SALE. It looked as if it had been there all along, the cardboard warped from the weather and flecks of rust along the metal rods. The sign looked as if it had endured a month or so of summer.

Like it had been there since the day we'd returned from Pittsburgh.

I glanced up the street to Mark's house. The Dysons' front door was shut, the windows were open but showed nothing. The house seemed normal.

I could hear voices inside our house, my Mom's among them, but the others I didn't recognize at all. They were laughing and talking loudly. I went in.

The bookcase was gone once more. The wall of the living room behind the couch was bare white. A couple—a young man and a very pregnant woman—were sitting there while my Mom sat in the chair across the coffee table from them, along with another older woman. They all looked at me.

"Rob," Mom said, her voice fast and bright with excitement, "this is Mr. and Mrs. Powers, and Mrs. Collins, their realtor. They've just made an offer on the house. I called your Dad in Pittsburgh and we've accepted." She over-smiled at me, her hands on the lap of her skirt, the Jackie Kennedy hairdo looking too perfect. I must have looked like an idiot, standing there with my mouth open, too stunned to speak. *Dad in Pittsburgh; accepted the offer...*I was feeling the vertigo again that I'd felt in the woods, that sense of rising panic.

"That's the price, and it's already been paid..."

"Look how dirty you are," Mom said to me, then smiled indulgently at the trio of strangers. "Rob's always playing in the woods," Mom said to them. "Boys can be so...well, perhaps you'll know for yourself very soon." She smiled at Mrs. Powers, who cupped the mound of her belly with her hands and smiled back. "Rob, why don't you go clean up? I'll have dinner ready in a bit..."

"Yeah, sure." I was glad for the excuse. I couldn't stand their empty smiles, couldn't bear the way they looked at me. I was afraid that if I stayed there any longer I'd start shouting at them. *"Can't you see how I've changed? Can't you tell the awful thing I've done? I've killed someone. I murdered Mr. Dyson, Mom. I killed him and I buried him in the woods…"*

The confession wanted to burst out of me, to tear out of my body in a scream my soul couldn't contain. "Good to meet you," I managed to blurt out. "Congratulations. I hope you like the house as much as we did," I told them, and half-ran for the bathroom. The hallway, the kitchen…the house looked more like a showpiece than a home, with everything cleaned up and polished and in its place. The sink in the bathroom was spotless, the fixtures gleaming.

I shut the door and sat on the toilet, my breath racing. I left the light off, sitting there in the gathering twilight, listening to the chatter in the living room and the first mutterings of thunder in the distance. I sat there until the first flickers of lightning painted the walls and I heard the mad drumming of rain on the awning.

There was a knock on the door not long after the thunderstorm passed, around eight or so. The western clouds had broken to reveal a purple evening. The streetlights were already on. "Can you get that, honey?" Mom asked me. "I'll start the dishes. You know, you've hardly eaten a thing…"

I pushed away from the table and went to the door. I recognized the form outside the rippled glass, and I hesitated, arranging my face before I opened the door. "Hey, Mark," I said.

"Hey," he answered. The right side of his face was badly bruised and swollen. He rubbed at it unconsciously as he stood there.

"You okay?" I asked him, and he scowled.

"Yeah. Look, uh, you haven't seen my dad, have you? Mom hasn't seen him since early this afternoon. He was cutting the grass, but he stopped and must've taken off somewhere. He didn't take the car, though; he must've walked. Then that storm came up and he still didn't come home, and…" He stopped. His eyes narrowed. "Man, what's up with you?"

The taste of acid lingered in the back of my throat. "Nothing," I told him. "I'm just…I'm not feeling real good right now. Got a stomachache."

He continued to stare at me as he nodded. "So…you seen my dad?" He looked past me, presumably to see if my Mom was within earshot. "I thought maybe he walked down the hill to Eddie's Tavern to get plastered, but Mom called there and they said he hasn't been there for a couple days. I think she's about ready to call the fucking pigs."

The secret in me swelled. I felt like my ribs were about to burst out from my skin.

"Mark, your dad…I saw what he did to you and he knew that I saw him. He came after me in the woods, he threatened me and he hit me, and I…I killed him, Mark. I had to do it—I had to do it to save myself, and to save you, too. I had to make things right for both of us. You understand that, don't you? You gotta understand…"

I thought the words. I composed them in my head. No matter how awful they were, it had to be better than holding all this in. But I saw *her* then—Sheila. She was standing in the gathering darkness, on the sidewalk past the front porch steps behind Mark. She looked at me, pleadingly. She shook her head. "No." I saw her mouth the word silently. Tears glistened on her cheeks, reflecting the porch lights. She steepled her hand in front of her mouth, her eyes stricken. She was still shaking her head.

I swallowed my confession instead. "Nah, I haven't seen him," I told Mark. I heard Sheila inhale audibly, and found myself surprised that Mark didn't turn to look at her too. He saw me looking past his shoulder and turned slightly, but Sheila had already slipped away, padding softly through the grass and around the side of the house into the night.

Mark looked back at me. I could see gathering suspicion in his eyes. I'd never been a good liar; I'd especially never been able to fool Mark with a lie before, had rarely even tried. "You *sure*, Rob?" he asked me. "You sure you haven't seen him?"

I tried to shrug but managed to lift only one shoulder.

"What'd you *do*, Rob?" he asked, his cheeks flushing so that the bruise stood out even more.

"Nothing," I answered. "I didn't do nothing. I mean, yeah, I did see your dad earlier today, I guess. When he was cutting the grass…"

Mark lifted his chin slightly, but he was still staring at me strangely. "Yeah. Dad just left the lawnmower in the back, with the yard half cut. Looks to me like he hopped the fence and went back into the woods for some reason, 'cause the weeds past the fence were trampled down. You wouldn't know the reason for that, would you?" He was glaring at me, and I struggled not to look away.

"No." I swallowed hard, so loudly I was sure Mark could hear it. "I just kinda caught a glimpse of your dad when I went out, that's all, and that's when he was still in the front yard. I was with Sheila. I didn't see…Didn't know…" I stopped.

His eyes held mine for a few long breaths, then finally dropped away again. "I'm going to get a flashlight and go back there and look around a bit—'fore Mom calls the cops. Maybe he twisted a leg or something and couldn't get back. You want to come help?"

I didn't. I wanted to stay here, wanted to retreat to my room and go to sleep, hoping that I'd wake up tomorrow back in a world that hadn't been turned upside down. But I was trapped in the lie and couldn't refuse.

"Yeah, sure," I told him. "Just let me get one of our flashlights and tell Mom what's going on…"

We spent an hour in the rain-soaked dark of the woods, the legs of our jeans soaked to above the knees from pushing through soaked brush and weeds, calling out "Mr. Dyson!" and "Dad!" so loudly that we shocked the night dwellers into silence. Ours were calls that I knew would never be answered. Mark circled deeper into the woods, closer and closer to the Seven Caves. I tried to change our movement, but couldn't lead him away without being obvious. In the end, I saw Mark's flashlight beam flicker over the wet, gleaming stones of the gateway. I shivered, seeing them, but the stones were clean and pale.

"Mark, man, your dad's not here. He would have heard us hollering by now. Let's head back, huh? I think my flashlight's about to give out."

He didn't answer. He waved his beam around. I saw the light touch a maple sapling just past the gateway, then the young tree's twin, alongside. For an instant, I thought I would see JD standing between them, resurrected like Kitty-Kitty. That would be all right, I thought. That would be fine. I'd accept that. I'd face down JD's ghost if it would show Mark the truth.

He wasn't there. Mark's beam illuminated nothing. "Shit," Mark said. He leaned against the column that Sheila and I had washed only a few hours before, the column that had crushed JD's skull. "Shit." There was a haunted emptiness in his face, exaggerated by the harsh light of my flashlight.

"Mark, you know, if…if he's gone…"

"What, Rob?" Mark flared, standing upright. "What do you mean, 'if he's gone'?"

I blinked, took a step back. "It's just…well…maybe that wouldn't be so bad, huh? You'd be safe from him, you and your mom and your sister. Isn't that what you wanted?"

He glared, hand clenched around the steel of his flashlight. "Shut up, Rob," he said.

"I saw you and him the last time, Mark," I told him. "I saw it, and…" The rest wouldn't come out. I could see Sheila's stricken face, her silent plea.

"You saw nothing," Mark spat. "Just shut up. If you're smart."

"Mark, I should have gone to the cops then, or at least my folks…"

"You don't understand," he interrupted me, his flashlight flaring in wild, bright arcs. The beam caught me in the eyes, so bright I had to shade them while spots danced before my eyes, fading from white to yellow to purple. "You really think I'll be *happy* if he's gone? You think that's what I want? I can't believe you'd even have it in your head that I don't want to find him. You think I *want* the cops poking around our house, asking me how I got these bruises or how my Mom got those marks on her arms, or why Jackie shrinks away if you lift your hand toward her or make a sudden move? Don't you think I'll always be wondering when he might walk back in the door, or if having him come back might be just what I want—part of me, anyway. He's still my dad, Rob. He's still…" He kicked at the leaves. He touched his swollen face. "God, you're so fucking stupid!"

JD wouldn't be coming back. At least I hoped not. But I didn't tell Mark that. Mark was watching me. "You said you wanted to kill him," I said. "You said you wanted him dead. I've heard you say that."

"Sure, I said that. I'll bet you've thought the same thing about your folks, too, when you're really pissed at them. It doesn't mean—" He stopped. Looked at me with his head cocked to one side. "What did you mean by that, Rob?" he asked. "What the fuck did you mean?"

I shook my head. "Nothing. I don't mean nothing."

He stared, silent. An owl hooted in the valley, dark wings thrashed overhead, unseen. Finally Mark gave an exasperated curse and strode off, without another word, without waiting for me. His flashlight beam slid over the ground, a halo.

I followed him back, pursued by ghosts.

CHAPTER TWENTY-FOUR

The police came eventually. They questioned Mark, his mom, and his sister. They came to our house and asked Mom and myself more questions—all of them pretty innocuous. They questioned Mark's family again: a lot more intensely, I think, since the detectives were in the house for hours. It was obvious from what they asked people and their tone that they thought JD had decided to skip town entirely. They searched the neighborhood and the woods, but not very thoroughly and without much support beyond a few neighbors. I 'helped,' again, tramping through the woods aimlessly, staying well away from the Seven Caves and my stomach churning the entire time, afraid that someone would come across the body and discover my secret.

Then, sometime the next morning, they called off the search and we heard nothing else.

Each day I woke up hoping things had changed, that somehow JD would have returned and the world would have somehow lurched back to the way it had been. It never did. I didn't see Mark much—he stayed in his house, mostly, and if he went into the woods, he went alone.

I didn't see Sheila either. She had vanished entirely. I wouldn't go back to the Seven Caves, but I walked the other paths in the woods, hoping to glimpse her and talk to her again, but she never appeared.

Two weeks later, the house packed, Mom and I followed the moving van on the long road to Pittsburgh. I hadn't seen Sheila since that night, and Mark only once or twice. Mark managed to get a job washing dishes at Maury's Restaurant, just a mile down the hill, a week after JD vanished—Maury had probably read the papers, knew that his dad was missing, and felt sorry for Mark—and with work and the investigation and everything else going on, Mark never seemed to be around, or he claimed to be too tired to come out whenever I knocked on his door.

I didn't even see him the morning we left. He'd already gone to work. I never had the chance to really say goodbye. Mom and Dad returned to Cincinnati overnight a month later to close on the sale of the house, but school had already started by then, and I stayed behind in Pittsburgh at a neighbor's house.

But the woods…The woods never left me.

I never forgot, though I tried. God, I tried. I tried to erase those memories with distance. I tried to erase them with work and with life, with friends and girlfriends, with high school, then college, with drugs and alcohol and work and the rest of life, and none of that worked.

Nothing could erase the memories. I never forget. Never.

I tried to erase that day with weeks and months and years, but the memories stayed back there in the inner dark, always there, always waiting for me in haunted dreams…

ONCE UPON A TIME...

know now that there's no forgetting. Not ever. Your past clings to you like an obsessed limpet, impossible to dislodge. It shapes you and it forces you to its paths. I knew that one day I'd have to come back here.

The past clings to you like forgotten pieces of paper thrust deep into a pocket. The next morning, I checked out of the motel and drove back up to the old neighborhood, parking the car where I'd parked the day before. As I stood in front of what used to be Mark's house, I pulled out one of those papers in my pocket—a scrap of yellow newsprint encased in clear plastic, from an ancient *Cincinnati Enquirer* newspaper that had landed on our lawn a few days before I left Cincinnati for Pittsburgh.

READING MAN STILL MISSING

Reading police are currently looking for Jason Dyson of North Crest Drive, missing since August 3rd. According to his wife, Mary Mc-Carthy Dyson, Mr. Dyson was last seen by her and their son Mark on the 3rd just after noon, in the kitchen of the house. At that time, he was wearing a Cincinnati Bengals T-shirt and jeans, and said he was going outside to "do some yard work." An hour or so later, Mrs. Dyson went to call him in for lunch and found the lawnmower abandoned in the middle of the backyard and Mr. Dyson gone.

Chief Gray of the Reading police department says that foul play is not suspected. Mr. Dyson had told several co-workers that he was unhappy both at home and work, and might one day "just pack up and leave." A search of the neighborhood and the nearby woods immediately following his disappearance turned up nothing. Chief Gray asks that anyone seeing a person fitting Mr. Dyson's description contact the Reading police.

There was another paper in my pocket: much folded, brittle and yellow with age, the ink from the cheap ballpoint pen that had written the words fading. I didn't even need to look at that one, even though I brought it out also. I knew I could have read it without looking even as I fumbled to open the stubborn, pressed creases.

After we moved to Pittsburgh, I wrote to Mark. I wanted to explain to him what had happened. I wanted to tell him everything.

But I didn't, of course. I couldn't put my confession down on paper, couldn't admit it. But I did write him, a few days after we arrived in Pittsburgh, sitting in my new room in my new house with all my old furniture looking as strange and uncomfortable in this new setting as I felt.

Mark: I know you and Sheila will get together now. Heck, maybe you'll even stay together, get married, and have kids who will play in the woods just like we did. I don't know. But I just want you to know that it's okay with me, Mark. Be with her. Love her. Make her happy—that's what matters the most to me, that she's happy. We both love her, and she loves both of us. But you're there now, and I'm not...

The letter was full of juvenile, maudlin angst and romanticism. I knew that even then, and I went on for far longer in that vein. I received a reply a week later, much shorter and far more succinct. Mark's few words were written on the decades-old paper I held in front of me now, with his old house as a backdrop.

What the hell are you talking about? Grow up, asshole; I'm done with all those games in the woods. Where's my Dad, Rob? That's all I want to know. Where the fuck is my Dad? Do you know where he is? If you do, tell me.

I never answered the letter. Mark never wrote me again.

Before I came back to town, I'd looked up the property records for Mark's house. His mom sold the house two years after we moved. It's been through another three owners since then. Mark's not even a ghost there anymore. I never did find out where the Dysons had moved to, or even whether Mark had moved with his Mom, since he'd have been almost eighteen at the time and maybe heading to college. I lost track of Mark, though I have to admit I didn't try all that hard. He'd never tried to contact me again; I never really made an effort to find him other than through some half-hearted googling. There are lots of Mark Dysons out there, after all, even if I did find out where he moved to, and I wouldn't know which of them he might be, if any.

Only...the truth is that I *could* have found him, if I'd really wanted to. A few judicious calls or e-mails or letters to some of those Mark Dysons, asking if they might be the Mark who had once lived on North Crest in Reading, Ohio, and one of them might have answered "yes." But I never did that. Maybe I didn't want to know what Mark might say to me. Maybe I didn't want to answer the questions he might have had. Maybe I didn't want to know what had happened to him and to Sheila.

The paper tore along one of the creases even as I tried to fold it back together. For a moment, I frowned, thinking that I had to repair it with a strip of cellophane tape. I was sure the motel manager could find some for me when I got back, then I realized that it didn't matter anymore. I wasn't going to see the motel manager, didn't need the tape, didn't even need to keep the paper at all. I even managed a half-smile as I let it drop into the gutter in front of the house. The newspaper clipping I put back in my pocket.

As I turned, I saw the man now living in Mr. Bell's house on his porch holding his bills, staring at me. I thought he might even say something about the dropped paper, but he didn't. I stepped on it as I started to walk back to the car, and he went into the house.

I wondered if Kitty-Kitty's bones were still buried in his front yard.

I looked again at the house that had once been mine. The Powers family, after buying the house from us, had kept it for ten years, then sold it themselves. The property was still held by the next owner. The current residents had built another addition on the back that I glimpsed as I walked toward it—an aluminum-sided extrusion that didn't match either the original house or my memory of it. There were toys in the front yard: a plastic tricycle, a big yellow baseball bat: so there were young kids in the neighborhood again, or maybe grandkids. I smiled at that, too. I remembered Mom telling me—when she came back for Mr. Bell's funeral four or five years after we left—that the old neighborhood didn't have kids anymore, that everyone who lived there seemed to be old.

There is rebirth. Everything cycles. At least I hoped so.

And the woods...They at least seemed semi-familiar as I walked down the side yard of our old house, opened the gate in the chain-link fence and went into the backyard at a quick walk. I was lucky—no one was there. I went to the back fence and put my hands on the top rail. I wondered if I could still do this, as I once had.

"Hey!" The man in Mr. Bell's house was at his back door now, scowling at me. "You! What are you doing back there?"

I didn't answer him. I bent my knees and pushed, my legs protesting, but I managed to clear the top bar, though the impact on the other side nearly staggered me. The man was still shouting and heading toward me. "I just want to see the woods," I told him. "I used to play back there." He looked uncertain but he halted as I went on into the sheltering embrace of the trees. That twisted oak over there; it had been there always, a little more overgrown with vines now than in my memory, with carved initials of strangers who came after us and who like us also abandoned the woods for adulthood. I wondered if they ever come back here. I wondered if they'd ever tried to regain the magic.

I wondered if *I* could.

In my time, the trails Mark and I had worn had been wide and deep. We'd thought them permanent, but I could see now how mistaken that was. In the intervening decade, the woods had reclaimed the ground. There was the ghost of a pathway at the edge of the bramble, and even that died a few strides in, terminating in a hollow filled with crumpled soda cans, torn potato chip and candy wrappers, cigarette butts, and a few empty beer bottles: a hideout for some teenagers' illicit drinking and smoking. Beyond was a hedge of snarled blackberry and honeysuckle which looked as if it had grown undisturbed for years. I pushed through, grunting with the effort and thinking how silly I must look, an old man flailing against the tenacious weeds.

I broke through, sweating and out of breath, and found myself on a slope I remembered—without any path, but relatively open. Just down a bit, I knew, was the small creek winding down to the greater bed of Cooper Creek. I started down the slope, holding onto young trees to avoid slipping in the slick leaves underneath, marveling at the smell—more than anything else, the odor of fallen leaves and green growth and cool earth brought back memories. Halfway down the hill, I saw a fallen log. I stopped there, tapping it once with a fallen branch. The sound was a dull plonk and the branch, rotten, broke in half at the first blow, but I could imagine a low *doom* reverberating as if I'd touched the skin of a huge drum, and the corners of my mouth lifted.

It took me three-quarters of an hour, altogether: down along the creek, past Salamander Hill and then east a bit and up once more to where the Seven Caves once bloomed. The "caves" were gone entirely, and I was navigating mostly on instinct and memory. I could just hear the sounds of the neighborhood, and so I moved deeper in until the sounds of suburbia started to fade.

And I saw it...

The two columns of Mark's "gateway" were covered now by vines, not even their sparkling granite tops exposed, and the trees beyond it that had once been saplings were taller and more imposing, but I recognized this place. A shaft of golden sunlight caressed one of the gateway columns, and I shuffled forward like a penitent treading up a church aisle until I could pull the vines away from the slabs of smooth mica-flecked stone. I leaned close, peering down at the matrix of colored minerals caught in the surface, looking for...

"You can still find the blood, if you look closely enough."

Oh, I'd hoped. Over the decades, I'd hoped and I'd prayed and I'd imagined. But still, the sound of her voice sent me staggering backward with a gasp, straightening guiltily. I looked past the gateway, to where twin maple trees rose to three times a man's height, their trunks now as thick as my arms. For a moment, I couldn't see anyone, then the shadows merged still deeper in the forest and I saw her.

Sheila.

She looked the same, her face still unmarred by any lines but for a faint crinkling of crow's feet at the corners of her eyes as she smiled. She was wearing what she'd worn the first day I'd seen her: jeans and a loose blouse. She put her hand on the right column of the gateway.

"Hey, Rob," she said. The light on her face dazzled. "It's been a long time."

I nodded, not trusting myself to say anything. My mouth was dry and I licked at my lips, swallowing hard, my breath sounding louder than anything else in the world. She swayed a step forward. Her feet made no sound on the ground. I had to force myself not to move back the same distance. "I knew you'd come back. I waited for you…"

"Sheila…" I began, my hands lifting. I stopped and let them fall back to my side. "God, I missed you. No one else…no one else ever meant as much to me. No one."

There were tears gathering in her eyes, sparkling in the erratic sun-shadow below the trees. "I know," she told me. "I'm sorry. I wish it had been different for you. I wish you could have been happy. But I was always here. I waited, but you never came."

"Did you and Mark…?" I asked, but she was already shaking her head into the question and I let the rest trail away.

"No," she said in a low voice of honey and milk. "I never saw Mark again after you left."

I started toward her, wanting to take her into my arms—wanting to feel the solidity and reality of her. But she backed away, shaking her head and bringing up a warning hand. "Not yet, Rob. Not yet."

"Why not?"

One of the tears swelled and slid down her cheek as she pressed her lips together in what was nearly a smile. She took a long breath. "Magic always has a cost," she said. "Surely you realize that by now." She gestured, and the vines curled away from the gateway stones as if they were green-leaved snakes, and the flat mounds were slick and wet and red, as I'd seen them the day that Mark had killed Kitty-Kitty, as bloodied as they'd been when JD had died here.

"Yes, I know," I told her, grimacing. I could feel my head pounding with the memories. "I've known that all along."

"I'll be waiting," she said to me. We were close enough that I could smell the mint of her breath, and she reached out to brush her hand against my cheek, the hand warm and so very real against the stubbled wrinkles there. "You know where to find me."

"I know." Her hand left my cheek, and she turned to walk away, the hand that had just touched my face sliding over the side of one of the columns. I watched her slip into the twilight of the woods, listening to the hush of her passage until I could neither see nor hear her at all.

Some time afterward...

I thought I heard a dog barking somewhere in the gloom of the woods. There was a fluttering overhead and a huge crow landed heavily on the crown of the column opposite me. It cocked its head, peering at me quizzically with a single bead-like eye, then cawed loudly. I realized that I was sitting uncomfortably slumped against one of the columns of the gateway and sat up. The crow hopped once, flapping its wings, then settled again with another caw before lifting heavily and flying a short distance away into the woods. The bird cawed again, looking back at me from a low branch as if waiting. I struggled to my feet and walked between the gateway columns, shivering at the cold snagged there, and glad when I walked out into a blade of sunlight once more. I could see, faintly, a path worn in the leaves—near where the crow waited. When it saw that I was on the path, the bird gave a cry that sounded like satisfaction and pushed off from the branch, flying deeper into the forest. I followed, knowing that this was where Sheila had gone: around a bowed and ancient oak, down the slope of the hill toward where Cooper Creak murmured sleepily and distantly in its stone bed. I passed a chestnut tree, with the scars of old blight cankers swelling its trunk, each of them now healed over. I touched the bark and heard a deep, slow song, a song I remembered...

She was waiting for me, smiling and radiant, near where the trail led off to the hidden grove of the chestnuts. The crow was sitting on her shoulder, patient. As I came toward her, stumbling a little on the path, Kitty-Kitty came barking out from the under-brush, her fur dotted with prickles and her red tongue lolling from her mouth. The dog sat in front of me, her head craning up toward me as if it had never been severed from its body. "About time, dearie," Kitty-Kitty said. "I was starting to wonder if you'd ever come. But *she* never doubted."

I was looking at Sheila. The dog barked once, as if laughing. "Yeah, go on," Kitty-Kitty said. "You don't care about me, anyway. It was always her."

I reached down and stroked her head once, then went to Sheila. She held out her hand as I approached. I laced my fingers with hers. I leaned toward her and we kissed. Her lips were warm and yielding, and there was a hunger to our embrace.

"Oh, for Chris'sakes, just get a room," Kitty-Kitty growled from alongside us after a few minutes, and Sheila broke away with a laugh.

"Come on," she said to me, her voice husky and the tears falling unashamedly down her face. I touched them, marveling. "Before it gets too late."

She took my hand again. The crow had already flitted away under the trees, and now Kitty-Kitty went barking after it, lumbering down the path toward the chestnut grove. I hesitated a moment, looking back at the woods and almost believing I could hear Mark and myself hollering as we ran through the shadows under the trees. I could feel the magic caught there, the terrible and beautiful magic that were one and the same.

Then I smiled and kissed Sheila gently once more.

I walked with her down the hidden path.